SEE YOU TOMORROW

The Parrish family seemed an ideally happy one: devoted parents concerned about the talents, ambitions and needs of their teenage children— Rod, Julia and Lucy. But behind the loving exterior was tension. To Julia her father's devotion was obsessive and stifling, and she rebelled against the fact that she could not fight it in case she upset him. And upsetting Alex was something the Parrishes had to avoid, for fear of sparking off another of his black depressions that led to weeks of illness and withdrawal. Julia—at seventeen still unsure of herself—longed for an extrovert family like her friends the Croxleys, with whom she spent as much time as she could, to the irritation and jealousy of her father.

At the end of one happy, summer weekend the unthinkable happens and Alex tries to kill himself. The effect on each member of the family is dramatic and surprising, with help coming not from the Croxleys, to whom Julia naturally turns, but from a complete stranger, Charlie, who has shared Alex's experience of feeling totally isolated from everyone around him.

See You Tomorrow

PEGGY WOODFORD

THE BODLEY HEAD
LONDON

For Walter

British Library Cataloguing
in Publication Data
Woodford, Peggy
See you tomorrow.
I. Title
823′.914 [F]   PR6073.0615/
ISBN 0-370-30716-X

Printed in Great Britain for
The Bodley Head Ltd
30 Bedford Square, London WC1B 3RP
by Redwood Burn Ltd, Trowbridge
First published 1979
Reprinted and bound in this format 1986

1

Even the Croxleys' front door had a special fascination for Julia. It was a worn brown, inset with panels of Victorian stained glass; there was a bird on each panel—on one a peacock, on the other a flamingo. Each bird was surrounded with painted flowers. From outside the house in daytime these birds were unnoticeable, but once you were inside the front door their colours glowed against the outside light. And of course at night, when the house was lit up, the birds were jewel-like. To Julia they were symbolic of the entrancing nature of the Croxley family.

'I love your birds.'

'They were the reason we bought the house.'

Oh, the Croxleys, the Croxleys; Julia felt they had everything her family (and any other she knew of) did not have. They were original, talented, interesting, full of life and colour—the list was endless. Ever since they had arrived in the area not so long before, Julia felt her own life had taken on a new dimension. When Carmen Croxley had joined her class everyone had immediately tried to cultivate her friendship. Carmen took this interest as her due, and to Julia's amazement settled on her as a friend; from that moment Julia's status rose appreciably. Carmen was a girl everyone noticed and remembered—strikingly pretty, intelligent and domineering. She had a brother at Oxford called Timothy, who was as fair as she was dark. The moment Julia met him, she decided he was the most beautiful young man she had ever seen and fell in love with him.

'He looks anaemic,' said Julia's mother, Nell.

'Perhaps he's just slightly albino.' Rod waited for his sister's explosion.

'Oh, for heaven's *sake*. He's not that pale.'

'And why is Carmen called Carmen? Very pretentious name, isn't it?'

Julia sighed. 'Her grandmother was called Carmen; she happened to be Spanish. So there's a good reason for it.'

'Oh. Well, I suppose Mrs Croxley does look a bit like a blousey Spanish lady herself.'

'I don't see why you have to be so rude about them, Rod.'

'It's just to counteract you raving on about them all the time.' He tweaked her ear.

'Shut up.'

'Children, children,' said Nell Parrish absent-mindedly. 'Actually, I think Amy Croxley is rather splendid-looking in her way.'

Amy Croxley was a potter and her husband Joe a columnist (he grew annoyed when he was called a journalist). Amy and Joe were open and friendly and treated Julia as if she were a contemporary. This added to the Croxley allure; Julia spent as much time as she could at their house.

'Your new friends will get tired of you,' said Alex Parrish.

'They don't mind how often I drop in. They said so. Amy likes people to drop in, she says it makes London seem more villagey.'

'Don't overdo it.'

Julia knew that her father resented her friendship. She was sure it was because she had found other adults she could talk to more freely than she had ever talked to Alex and Nell. It was their fault; they never took her seriously.

'I *won't* overdo it. I'm not that insensitive.' She found a latchkey and began to go out. 'I'll see you later.'

'Where are you going?'

'To lunch with the Croxleys; Mum said I could.'

'I need your help in the garden. Besides, today is Sunday.'

Julia gazed wordlessly at her father, twisting the key round and round her finger.

'You see them every day of the week. I would have thought Sunday lunch was a time for the family. Your *own* family.'

'I'll come back early—'

'Really, Julia, it's too much. You spend every available moment in that house. You obviously prefer their company to ours—'

'Oh, Dad, don't be ridiculous. I don't—'

'Alex, dear, let her go. I said she could.' Nell appeared. 'She'll come back early and help you with the garden. She's made a lovely friendship, let her enjoy it.'

'I've no objection whatever to lovely friendships. But I was counting on her help today; Rod can't because of his revision, and Lucy's just not so efficient. Anyway I need both girls if I'm going to finish that paving.'

'I'll help you.'

'Why should you? You've got plenty to do already.' There was a pause.

'Well, you'll be pleased to hear that the Croxleys are about to go away on holiday,' burst out Julia. 'In fact this may be the last time I see them before they go.'

Alex went to the garden door before he replied: 'I hope it will give you an opportunity to get them into perspective.' He went out.

Nell sighed. Julia sighed. She met her mother's eyes.

'Shall I not go?'

'Don't be silly, darling. He's just being unreasonable.'

'He is beastly about them.'

'I can't think why. They seem a charming family to me.'

'It's not a bad patch starting again?'

'No. I'm sure it isn't. He's just tired and bad-tempered. Overworked.'

'That's how the last bad patch started.'

'I know, but Alex is basically so much better that it's not the same.'

Julia was reassured.

'You go off now, but come back early, won't you. I'm sure Alex will be in a better mood by then.'

Julia bicycled to the Croxleys, eager to see them and forget her demanding and possessive father. When she got to the house and rang the bell, no one appeared. She pressed her face to the glass birds and could see that the double doors into the garden were open. Faint sounds of music could be heard. Clearly the Croxleys were all in the garden. She rang again; no reply. Five minutes went by and she wondered how to attract their attention.

Stupidly, she felt tears rising. Then the telephone started to ring; surely they would hear that; they had bells fixed all over the house. She peered through the glass, and saw Amy run in. She allowed a minute or two to pass, and then pressed the bell firmly twice. She heard Amy shout: 'Just coming,' and felt relief pour through her.

'Oh. Julia.' Amy looked blank.

'You asked me to lunch.'

'Yes, of course. Do come in. Awful of me, I'd completely forgotten. Everyone's sunbathing in the garden. Carmen, here's Julia.'

'Hi.' Carmen stood up. She was wearing a bikini; her body was curved and full, but not plump. It was the sort of figure which men's magazines presented as the ideal. Julia felt a pang of envy; then the envy changed to panic as another voice said:

'Hullo, Julia.'

Timothy was lying on a lilo, a book in his hand. Julia stumbled down the last two steps, and almost fell over. She blushed.

'Hullo. I . . . I didn't know you were going to be here.'

'Came for the day on a sudden impulse.'

Carmen prodded him with her foot. 'I bet a girl-friend let you down and you had nothing better to do.' She opened a deckchair for Julia.

'Be quiet, infant.' He yawned. 'I just wanted a break from my hectic social life.' He returned to his book. Beyond him lay his father, snoring gently.

Julia sat in silence, miserably aware of Timothy and unable to think of anything to say.

'You should have brought your swim-suit,' said Carmen.

'Never mind.'

'I'd lend you one of mine, but it wouldn't fit you; you're such a little sparrow.'

'There speaks the elephant,' said Timothy without looking up from his book. Carmen ignored him. Julia sat feeling hot and over-

8

dressed, while Carmen stretched out beside her. Compared with Carmen, she was totally unattractive; however much Timothy teased his sister, the fact remained she was a beauty. Julia leant back in her chair and shut her eyes. Her mind felt jammed by Timothy's presence; all the ease she usually felt when with the Croxleys departed.

Amy came out with a jug full of juice and ice cubes, and glasses. She picked some mint and crushed it roughly before putting it into the jug. She then put an ice-cube on Joseph's chest. He shot upright.

'What beast did that?'

'Your dear wife.' Carmen tittered. 'Goodness, you've gone red, Joe. Watch out. Have some of my oil.' She held out the bottle but her father ignored it.

'Hullo, Julia. Or were you here before I went to sleep? Sun does confuse one.'

'I've just come.'

'Timothy, you rude oaf, stop reading and talk to us.'

'You've shown no great desire yourself for talking so far.'

'Refreshed by a sleep and stimulated by the sight of our guest, conversation is what I want now.' Joe was small and thin, quite the slightest member of his family. He had a thick mat of grey springy hair which stuck out all over his head, mop-like. This gave him an odd appearance; without his hair he would not have drawn the eye at all.

'Actually, Julia, I wanted a word with you; I wanted to pick your brains for an article.'

Julia looked at him in surprise.

'I'm examining the role of patronage of the arts in our modern world, and something you said about your father's job came into my mind. What does he do precisely? Refresh my memory.'

'He's a sort of co-ordinator. He puts artists of all sorts in touch with people and organizations who might want to use them.'

'So for instance he could promote the artists he liked by gently pushing commissions their way?'

9

'I don't know how much special power he has. For instance, there's one sculptor he doesn't like at all who often gets work; he's mentioned him because he can't understand why people choose him.'

'And he's employed by the local authority to offer this invaluable service?'

'Yes.'

'Wonders will never cease. A modern version of the patron. Do you think he'd be willing to talk to me about his job?'

'Oh yes, I'm sure he would. He loves talking about it.' Then doubt filled her; Alex was so unpredictable.

'Just what I need. The civil service at local level as patron of the arts. Presumably if the Sewage Department wants a sculpture he puts them in touch with suitable artists?'

'I think so . . . I'm not very clear about the details.'

'I can just imagine what sort of piece the Sewage Department would commission,' said Carmen, beginning to giggle.

'Your sense of humour is as infantile now as it was when you were five,' said Timothy. Carmen took no notice and continued to giggle.

Joseph talked on about the history of art patronage, its importance (Timothy disagreed) and the effect of its wane. As Julia listened, she thought : this is why I like this family; they *talk* about things, *do* things and discuss them as well, and I learn something new every time I come here. Dad never talks to us about his work or the interesting people he meets. And Mum hasn't got anything interesting to talk about anyway. Well, that's not fair, but—

'She's dreaming.'

'Oh, sorry. What did you say?'

'Would your father mind if I gave him a ring sometime today? I know it's Sunday, but I've got a deadline.'

'I don't think he'd mind you ringing on a Sunday.'

If he minded, it would be the question not the fact that it was posed on a Sunday. 'Shall I ask him to ring you when I get back?' Perhaps she could then prepare the way.

'No, for heaven's sake, why should he be troubled. I'll call him later.'

Joseph yawned, showing gold teeth, and ran his hands through his hair. 'Amy darling, will you cut my hair? In this heat I swelter.'

'It'll rain if you do.' Carmen was still laughing to herself. 'She only cuts it once a year. Like a sheep-shearing.'

'I'll do it now. Come, let's wet it. The hose is over there.'

Amy made him bend over while she soused his head. Then she combed the wet hair downwards all round his face and ears, making him look quite extraordinary. She cut his hair with a large pair of dressmaking scissors, taking very little care. Joseph, unconcerned, talked on about Renaissance Italy.

'You have the typical journalist's mind,' said Timothy. 'You master the superficialities of a subject and hold forth as if you know it all. People with real knowledge keep quiet because they've reached the stage of realizing how little they know.'

Joe laughed. 'A little knowledge is a dangerous thing. Why don't you say it, my wise, well-educated son? I didn't go to Oxford, of course. That makes me suspect at once.'

'Going to Oxford has nothing to do with it.'

'Oh, don't let's go over this well-worn track,' said Amy, throwing down the scissors.

'I couldn't agree more.' Timothy went back to his book; Joe made a funny face for Julia's benefit. As his hair dried it rose again in a halo round his head. Grey curls started to blow round the garden. The Croxleys' garden was a wilderness of downtrodden grass and unweeded beds. A huge Albertine rose encroached from one wall over half the garden, and its mass of blooms were deliciously scented. But once its flush of flowers was over, it was a spiny, energetic growth for the rest of the year, and nothing else in the garden had much in the way of flowers, choked by weeds as it all was. The only edible thing the garden produced was mint, which was rampant and had ousted other herbs.

After lunch Timothy disappeared. Julia sat on, gossiping to Carmen, knowing she ought to leave but hoping he would reappear. She was aware of his absence as strongly as she was of his presence.

'Julia.' Joe stood at the garden door, holding the extension phone in his hand. 'What's your home number? I thought I might give your father a ring if you think now is a good moment.'

'Oh, yes. He's at home.' Joe sat down on the step with the phone beside him and dialled the number he was given. Alex answered it himself.

'Mr Parrish? Joseph Croxley speaking. I have your delightful daughter here, and she tells me you might be willing to talk to me about your work. I'm writing some articles on the rôle of patronage —no, no, I realize you're not a patron in the old sense—'

Julia could see from Joseph's expression that her father was being awkward.

'Perhaps I could come and see you to hear in greater detail what you do—no, I'm sure it would be most helpful, your job is exactly what I need—'

There was a longish pause during which Alex said something which clearly annoyed Joe. 'Of course. If that's the way you'd prefer it. I always find conversation more useful—no, I quite understand. Yes. Yes. I'll pass the message on.' He put the phone down. 'He says he'd be grateful if you'd hurry home as he needs your help in the garden.'

Julia stood up, miserable, wishing the earth would swallow her. 'Doesn't he want to help?'

'He has suggested I prepare a list of questions and send them to him. He will then write something for me later this week. Of course I haven't time to wait for written answers. So I'll have to do without his valuable help. And it would have been valuable.'

'I'm terribly sorry—'

'My dear child, why should you be? He's got a right to refuse information.' Joe saw the expression on Julia's face and patted her shoulder. 'I obviously caught him in a bad mood. If he changes his mind, let me know.' Joe winked and took the telephone back to the study.

Julia bicycled home, fuming with rage and humiliation. How dare her father be so mean and unfriendly. He didn't seem to care about anyone but himself. She wanted to scream at him, shake him. What made her specially angry was the fact that there was nothing she could do : a full-scale row with her father was impossible, forbidden. Alex suffered from periodic depressions, and they were so frightening that any family tension which could trigger them off was squashed before it could begin. Their family life went into cold storage when Alex was ill; life became limbo until the cloud lifted again.

The frustration Julia felt boiled over when she saw her mother cutting the front hedge. It didn't need cutting; Nell was there to catch her before she went into the house, to calm her down and take the tension onto herself. Julia was tempted to bicycle straight past her house.

'Ju. Stop.'

'I'm stopping.'

'Now listen, I know it's upsetting—'

'Yes, yes, I know. Calm down dear, don't aggravate your father any more—'

'Julia.'

'If it's any comfort to you I won't give him the pleasure of seeing I'm angry. But I could murder him, I really could—why was he so rude to Joseph Croxley?'

'Darling, you know he's prejudiced about the Press in general, and says they misrepresent everything. That's the only reason he didn't want to be interviewed; I'm sure there's nothing personal in it.'

'He hates the Croxleys.'

Nell started snipping at the hedge. 'He doesn't hate them. Don't exaggerate. They're not his type particularly, but that's nothing serious. You mustn't take all this so much to heart.'

Julia gazed at her mother's calm face. She was sure neither of her parents understood the special nature of her friendship with the Croxleys.

13

'Alex is very tired at the moment. Helping to set up an index of local craftsmen, plus the special exhibition at the Town Hall has been a great drain on him. You must help him relax at weekends. It wasn't particularly wise of you to encourage Mr Croxley to ring him up on a Sunday.'

'Working like a fiend in the garden is hardly relaxing.'

'He finds it so. Hard physical work is a great restorer of the mind.'

Julia moved off; it was the final straw when her mother started moralizing. She put her bicycle in the shed built at the side of the house and went inside to change into old clothes before going to help her father.

Alex greeted her with a beaming smile.

'Hullo, my love. That was quick. Look how much we've done.'

He was friendly, accommodating, and though full of conversation did not mention Joseph Croxley. After an hour of spreading and smoothing sand as a base for the paving stones, Julia said casually:

'You weren't exactly helpful to Mr Croxley.'

'Why should I be?' Alex was affable and relaxed. 'I dislike being pumped for superficial information. He's only writing ephemera, anyway.'

Julia thumped the sand down with her spade, her face averted. Arrogant so-and-so, she thought. But all she said was:

'He writes for a very good paper.'

'No paper is very good; it can't be. Some are better than others, and his is better than most. I can't imagine how anyone can find writing for the mass media anything but a demoralizing job. In the long run, at all events. Don't you agree?'

Julia was in no mood for a discussion, particularly about journalism. 'Is that sand spread evenly enough?'

'Yes. Except for that hillock there.'

Julia smoothed it so energetically she went through to the earth below and had to start again.

'Anyway,' Alex went on, 'I agreed to answer in writing any questions he cared to send me. That seems helpful enough.'

14

'He said he had a deadline and wouldn't possibly have time to wait for your reply. I think he needed to see you today or to-morrow.'

Alex laughed. 'That backs up what I was saying about journal-ists—butterflies producing ephemera. Always in a rush. Always expecting the other man to fall over himself to fit in with their deadlines. There's something insulting about it.'

'Joe wasn't at all insulting—'

'You don't understand what I mean.'

Nell came up, offered tea, and took Julia away with her to help. 'Did you ask Carmen back for tea?'

'You must be *joking*.'

'Now, Julia, stop over-reacting. You're still angry about this silly business and it's quite unnecessary. I'm sure the Croxleys haven't given it another thought.'

'I bet they have. Joe wanted—'

'Listen to me. They may fill your mind all day long, but you can be sure you don't fill theirs. Give over, Ju.' Nell hesitated, aware she was hurting her daughter. 'A lot of people find it un-pleasant if you care too much about them and they . . . stop wel-coming you.'

Julia did not reply. Rod came in after a few minutes, stretching and yawning. 'What a waste of a beautiful day to sit poring over revision.' He yawned again. 'Really, I must be mad to do four A-levels in one go.'

'Think how nice it will be if you pass them all.' Nell piled things onto a tray.

'Oh, I'll pass them all, but I want to get credits.' Rod spoke matter-of-factly. He was an excellent scientist and mathematician. 'The trouble is I simply haven't had time to cover the complete syllabus.' He yawned yet again, and rubbed his pale freckled face. 'What I'd really like is a hard day's walking in rough country. My head feels quite addled.'

'Come and help me heave paving stones,' said Alex from the doorway. 'That should clear away some of your cobwebs.'

'I'm going to.'

'I've just got tea ready.' Nell stood holding the tray.

'We'll have it in a minute. Take it to the end of the garden and we'll join you.' But by the time Alex and Rod did, the tea was cold.

2

The weather was hot, so hot that Julia had to move out of the sun under the mulberry tree. The heat wave had begun the day the Croxleys had gone on holiday; ten days later the temperature was still in the eighties. Julia lay doing nothing; weekends felt empty without her friends; she wondered if Carmen missed her.

'Julia.'

Her father's voice floated through the heat. She did not answer; it was even too much to slap at the fly that was tickling her leg.

'Ju! Aren't you coming?'

Coming where ... oh yes, Alex was taking them to some exhibition. Too hot, too hot.

'Julia. Wake up.'

'I'm not really asleep.'

'Aren't you coming?'

'It's so hot. It seems a pity to waste this lovely sun.'

Alex came into the garden towards her.

'Don't be ridiculous. You can sunbathe any time. This is the last day of the exhibition.' He prodded her with his toe.

'I can't bear the thought of streets and heat and people.' Julia gazed through half-closed eyes at the web of leaves above her. 'Sorry, Dad.'

Alex stared at his daughter's thin body in its blue denim bikini. 'You're a damned fool, Ju. A collection of Cranachs like this might never be seen again.'

'My loss.'

'Indeed. Foolish child. Rod and Lucy are coming.'

Peace descended on the garden. Julia gazed up mesmerized at the fluttering leaves above her. The mulberry tree was large and old; it had once been part of a park which was developed into a

17

housing estate in 1903 by an Edwardian speculator who had had the sense to keep the trees. This tree was at least two hundred years old, and possibly much older. The original great house had been Elizabethan, but its exact site was now lost. The mulberry tree was an intrinsic part of the Parrishes' life; it still cropped well, and wine and preserves were made each year in abundance.

'Julia.' Nell's voice made her jump. 'I thought you'd gone with the others.'

'I decided not to.'

'Oh, Julia. You could have made the effort.'

Nell had gardening gloves and gumboots on, and looked very hot and dirty. 'He was on such good form this morning. You being difficult could annoy him for days. I could shake you.' Wearily she returned to her weeding again.

After a while Julia turned over and reached for her book. Her reading progressed very slowly. Some insect gave her a vicious bite on the arm; then the telephone rang, and she stubbed her toe on the doorstep as she ran in to answer it. The call was from one of Lucy's friends. Irritated, she returned to her sunbathing. But the pleasure was gone; her mood had slipped from indolence to boredom. The boredom became guilt when she saw Nell wheeling a barrow piled high with weeds. She got up to help. Nell's face was red and shiny with sweat as they tipped the barrow out onto the compost heap behind the garage. Nell leant against the wall.

'Ouf. What heat.'

'That's why I didn't go with Dad. I hate crowded places in the heat.'

'It was an exhibition not to be missed, you know.'

'Why didn't you go then?'

'I've been twice already. I just couldn't get Alex to go until the last day. Typical.'

She tidied up the edge of the compost heap; green ooze flowed gently. There was a rich rotting smell. 'I just wish you'd gone, darling. To see the pictures, and because it upsets Alex so much when you children refuse to join in with his plans. I know he's possessive about you, but there we are.'

'He didn't seem very annoyed.'

'Perhaps I fuss too much.' Nell took off her gardening gloves and undid her shirt to retrieve a piece of twig. 'He's been so much better recently, I ought to feel easy in my mind.'

'Don't you?'

Nell cleaned earth off her tools before replying. 'How can I, Ju? It's a fact of my existence. Alex goes into a black depression for five, six, eight weeks, and neither I nor anyone seems able to help him. We all live a miserable life while he's like that, and then for no particular reason he's better again. I'd feel so much happier if only he'd go to a doctor.'

'But he's been to Doctor Railton.'

'I mean a proper psychiatrist. Railton's a dear, but he's just a GP, and even he admits that he's not capable of dealing with mental illness. He just prescribes Valium and of course Alex hates their effect and throws them away.'

'He said you threw them away once.'

'Well perhaps I did. They're no answer. But I've asked Alex again and again to see a psychiatrist, and he won't. So there we are.' Nell coiled the hose expertly. 'He says we ought to be able to sort out our own mental problems, and in a way he's justified—he drags himself out of his depressions eventually. Eventually.'

Julia stood remembering a Christmas holiday when her father had shut himself away in his study, hardly speaking to anyone for two weeks. He had prepared no presents, and Julia felt the pang of this even now.

'That Christmas was dreadful.'

'Dreadful. The trouble is, while his illness is beginning he won't accept that it is, and when he's ill he's totally unapproachable, and when he's better he says: Look, I'm all right again—why should I go to a shrink when I can do it myself.' Nell shut her eyes and sighed. Then she took the shears and began to cut the hedge. 'But I'm sure I fuss too much. He's had a great deal of pressure recently, and apart from being very tired he's fine. Yes, I fuss too much.' Showers of privet fell at her feet. Julia stood watching.

'I'm sorry I didn't go with him today.'

'Cook us a nice dinner instead.'

Julia had a natural knack with food, and enjoyed cooking. Yet nothing depressed her more than the fact that everyone urged her to take up cooking as a career since she was so good at it. I don't want to make cooking my career, she would wail. I can't think of a worse prospect.

There was a leg of lamb in the fridge, and she reached for her favourite recipe book to find some ideas. As she was collecting possible ingredients Alex, Rod and Lucy returned. From the expression on Rod's face, the expedition had had its drawbacks. Julia winked at him under cover and got a roll of the eyes in reply. Alex talked enthusiastically about the Cranachs.

'Superb. Superb. I haven't seen such a thrilling exhibition in years. If ever.' He took one of Julia's arms and examined it with exaggerated attention. 'But you do look a bit browner.'

Julia flapped the recipe book in his face. 'Watch out or I'll poison the dinner.'

'Even I liked it, non-visual animal though I am,' said Rod. 'I found it a breathtaking exhibition.'

Julia felt angry with herself. She flipped over the pages restlessly.

'Oh, well. Silly me for missing it. Did Lucy like it too?' Lucy had already gone to ring up the friend who had called earlier.

'She said she adored it.' Some of the enthusiasm faded from Alex's face. 'Where's Nell?'

'Still gardening.'

'For heaven's sake—she's been at it all day. I'm going to stop her.' He went into the garden. Rod cut himself a vast slice of cake and sat on the kitchen table.

'What went wrong?' asked Julia.

'Oh, nothing specific. You know how annoying it is when somebody will insist on talking when you want to absorb things in peace. Alex was in a commenting mood, so comment we got. It's mean to resent it because the comment was fascinating in itself.

Dad's so surprisingly knowledgeable.' He examined what was left of his piece of cake. 'This cake is distinctly stale.'

'I think it was destined for the birds.'

'Tell me now.' He threw the remains onto the lawn. 'Alex is so lively and communicative at the moment it seems churlish to resent anything.'

'I don't know, Rod. I think it shows how well he is that we're not pussy-footing with him all the time in the way we used to.'

Rod gazed at her. 'Could be. Could be.' He rubbed his hands through his wiry reddish hair. 'Oh God, I must go and do some work. I get butterflies every time I think of those exams.' As he passed Lucy giggling and chattering in the hall Julia heard him say : 'One of these days you're going to grow a receiver instead of an ear.'

'Oh clever.' Lucy made a rude noise before she returned to her conversation. 'No, it's just my dear witty brother.'

Lucy's voice grated on Julia. Lucy had a slight lisp, attractive to strangers but maddening to her family because they suspected she cultivated it. When teased about it, Lucy just smiled and continued to lisp. She was pretty in a pre-Raphaelite way, and had that typical faintly mysterious quality about her expression. It could hide depth or stupidity, said Rod, and you could never be sure which.

Lucy finished talking and wandered into the kitchen.

'Peel the spuds, Lucy, will you.'

'In a minute.'

Lucy stood leafing through the newspaper, looking for the woman's page. She was taller than Julia, and graceful where Julia was awkward. She had a natural sense of chic, and took greater care of her clothes, nails and hair than Julia ever did.

'I didn't know you had new shoes.'

'Oh these.' Lucy wriggled her foot around. 'I saved up for ages to buy them. They are nice, aren't they?'

'Bet they were expensive. They're super, though.' Julia sighed. Lucy chose her things so well; Julia always made mistakes. She had no clear idea of what suited her, whereas Lucy seemed to know instinctively. 'Next time I go shopping for clothes or shoes you must come with me and help me choose. I always seem to end up with something in a colour that matches nothing, or doesn't suit me, and if Mum comes she just flusters me.'

'Oh.' Lucy looked surprised. 'OK.'

'You don't sound particularly enthusiastic.'

'Well, hanging about while other people do their shopping isn't much fun.' She smiled vaguely as she spoke; as far as she was concerned, she was stating the obvious with no sense it might hurt. Other people's feelings were not particularly interesting to Lucy. She was oblivious rather than cruel, whereas Julia was oversensitive both to the effect of her remarks on others, and of theirs on her.

'Don't bother, then. I expect eventually I'll learn by my mistakes.'

Nell came in from the garden and began to wash the dirt off her hands and arms.

'I must have a bath.'

'Mum, can I go to Betty's now? She's just asked me.'

Nell hesitated. 'Julia's cooking us a special dinner.'

'Betty says I can have something to eat there.' Lucy was wholly uninterested in food. 'Please, Mum. I do so want to hear a new record she's just bought.'

'I suppose you can. Be back at the usual time.'

'Can I borrow your bike, Ju? Mine's got a puncture.'

'Why don't you mend your puncture. You've had it for ages. I'm fed up with you borrowing my bike.'

'I'll walk then.' Lucy began to go upstairs.

'Borrow my bike, for goodness sake.'

Lucy did not answer, but a little while later Julia heard the clatter of her bicycle being pushed out of the gate.

The pile of potatoes sat in the sink waiting to be done. To hell with Lucy, thought Julia; she gets out of everything. Nell peeled them instead, with practised speed.

'Now I think I'll go and have that bath. I feel disgustingly sweaty and dirty.' She put her arm round Julia's shoulders. 'What are you cooking?'

'Lamb provençale. Lots of garlic and tomatoes.'

'Lovely. Clever old thing.' She squeezed Julia's shoulders and left. Julia had begun to notice that she only touched her children spontaneously when she was happy. When Alex was ill, she barely even kissed them goodnight. She seemed to recoil from all contact. In fact the Parrishes as a whole were not a very demonstrative family, unlike the Croxleys who were for ever touching each other in casual affection.

Julia put the lamb into the hot oven of the Aga cooker and then stood indecisively. She noticed her father was standing in the middle of the lawn near the mulberry tree. He stood so still that his body had an eerie quality, that perfect stillness achieved by great mimic artists. Julia watched him, waiting for him to break his frozen stillness. She had no idea what his mood was because she could not see his face. The trance continued for some time; then Alex suddenly clapped his hands together as if to wake himself up. He came into the house looking tired, although his expression brightened when he saw Julia.

'I love that tree,' she said.

'I rather fear it.'

'But I've heard you say you love it like a member of the family—'

'Fearing something does not stop one loving it.'

They did not eat the lamb until quite late, because it took much longer to cook than Julia expected. The unaccustomed late hour, the warm night, the sudden happy mood which descended on everyone, made the atmosphere magically good. Nell, who had a beautiful soprano voice which she hardly ever used now, sang while she was in the bath. The sound filled Alex, Rod and Julia with quiet happiness, and thus the family mood was set. Nell appeared in a long simple cotton dress which, though old and much washed, made her look beautiful.

'That's my favourite dress,' said Alex. 'I shall be sad when it wears out.'

Julia too had changed out of jeans, because while basting the lamb she had spilt fat all down them. She was about to put on another pair when she saw her mother in the garden bending in her long dress to tie back a rose. She put down her jeans and wore a long skirt instead.

Rod had been sent to the off-licence to buy wine and on the way back met Lucy with Betty in the street.

'You're missing a party. Everyone's in a marvellous mood. Why don't you come back?'

Lucy hesitated. 'Betty too?'

'Betty too.'

Rod ushered the two girls in by saying: 'I picked up these two choice birds at a street corner. Thought they'd add to the party spirit.'

The girls giggled.

'Hey, you're all dressed up.' Lucy looked at her mother and sister accusingly.

'You're always dressed up, so why worry.'

'Girls, girls.' Nell waved her glass. 'Anyone who spoils the fun pays a fine. No arguments, sarcastic comments or other sabotaging activities, please.'

Julia caught her mother's eye. She was an adept at resisting the prevalent mood; now she grinned and said: 'OK. Pax.'

'Don't tell me you're becoming a social animal at last.' Alex's tone was light.

Julia prodded the lamb with a skewer before she answered. 'I am a social animal already. I wouldn't spend all that time with the Croxleys if I wasn't.'

Nell laughed. '*Touché.*'

'The lamb is done. We can eat.'

'I'm ravenous.' Rod prowled about, lifting the lids off saucepans. 'Lovely grub.'

'We've eaten already.'

'Well, you girls can watch us.'

'Oh, fun.' But Lucy and Betty were clearly enjoying themselves. They sat on the window-sill, talking together.

Alex lifted his glass high. 'To us all. I have a feeling the rest of this year is going to be good for everybody. Rod, you're going to pass your exams so brilliantly universities will clamour to have you—'

'Don't tempt fate.'

'No, I mean it. You, Julia, will discover what you're really best at and will never say again "I'm no good at anything except cooking".'

'That'll be the day.'

'And you, Lucy, you, Lucy—' Alex stopped, gazing at his youngest daughter. 'Do you know, I haven't a clue what you most want.'

'Life.' Lucy giggled.

'All right. You Lucy, will get Life in the measure you wish it.'

'And I wish Father Christmas would get on with the carving,' said Nell. 'The meat's getting cold.'

Alex picked up the carving knife and fork and waved them in the air. His mood of euphoria increased. 'Now don't be a wet blanket, Nell. Surely you must all know that sense of powerful intuition one gets sometimes. It's irrational, but often justified.' He plunged the fork into the meat.

'When I get light-headed about things they inevitably go horribly wrong.'

'Rod, Rod. Nothing will make you into a romantic.'

Rod laughed. He had the most attractive face when he laughed, although in repose his face was almost ugly. His laugh was deep and infectious. 'Actually, I will admit to a sneaking feeling that things are going to turn out rather well.'

'I think you're all tempting Providence,' said Nell. 'It makes me nervous.'

'Well, I'm not getting rosy intimations of my future, if it's any comfort to you,' said Julia. 'All I can see ahead is muddle, murk and gloom. I haven't a clue what I could do as a career; the only thing I'm good at I don't want to do, and things I'd love to do like the piano I'm no good at.'

'Go on. You're a good little musician.' Alex carved busily and did not meet her eye. 'And you work so hard at it.'

'That's the point. It's so depressing because I practise hard and all I do is become a little more competent. I get so angry that all my effort doesn't work a miracle, but it doesn't. I just haven't got that special spark.' Julia's eyes flashed.

'Well, if it's any comfort, Ju, I couldn't begin to apply myself in the way you do,' said Rod.

'You don't have to. You're cleverer than I am.'

'I'm not sure staying power isn't a better quality to have.'

'I'm sure I'd play better if I had more brain.'

'Have some more wine instead.' Nell topped up her glass. 'I shouldn't worry so much about it. If it's technique you lack, you'll probably acquire it, and if it's experience, well, give yourself time. All artists have to develop.'

'But Mum, you've missed the point. I don't think I've got the spark, the real talent. So what is there to develop?'

'Time will tell.'

'Time won't. Julia's right, I suspect.' Alex finished carving and moved the messy remains of the joint off the table. 'Experience ripens talent but it doesn't produce it. Look at all those young pianists we saw competing on television the other day; they haven't got maturity, but they've got everything else already.'

'Exactly, Dad.'

'Well, darling, don't make yourself unhappy about it—'

'But I'm not unhappy about it, Mum. The piano's a blind alley as far as I'm concerned, and I've faced that fact.' She knocked the gravy over. 'Blast.'

'Save that sublime sauce,' Alex wailed.

'There's more on the Aga.' Julia wiped up the spill and refilled the gravy-boat. As she sat down again Rod lifted his glass: 'To Julia, who cooks divinely, even if her Chopin falls short of perfection.' Julia growled at him, pleased. They all ate in silence for a while until Alex said: 'Let's light some candles. Where will I find them?'

He hummed as he dug some candle-ends out of a drawer and stuck them onto saucers. They continued their dinner by candle-light and silence descended again, but with no decrease in the general mood of happiness. Julia found the words 'love descending

26

breaks the air' floating through her mind; she could not remember where the words came from but it did not matter. They remained in her mind like a thin trail of light.

The magic evening continued. Nell gazed round her family with love. The high days and holy-days are never like this, she thought, when this is what they should be. I pray that everyone will behave with perfect charity on a special day, say Christmas Day, and they never do. They never do. And look at Alex; I can't remember when I last saw him so euphoric. And it's not a manic euphoria either. He's too relaxed. I do profoundly believe he's better.

'Nell's looking broody.'

'I'm not—I was just having some nice thoughts.'

'Let's play cards after supper.'

'Oh yes, let's. Or Monopoly.'

'No, Lucy, not Monopoly, for heaven's sake. I'm going to bed if you all play Monopoly.' Rod liked games where chance played as small a part as possible.

'Whatever we do, let's leave all this mess till the morning.' Nell pushed her chair back. They all gazed at her in surprise. She usually insisted on leaving the kitchen tidy. They danced in a line, hands on the hips in front, with Lucy leading, into the sitting-room, and scattered laughing onto the sofa and chairs. It was some time before they organized themselves into a game.

Later, when Nell and Lucy and Betty (with permission to stay the night) had gone to bed, the other three went to have a beer in the kitchen. Alex and Rod stood drinking from cans and Julia sipped a glass of orange in a companionable silence. Rod belched; the fridge whirred.

'I'm thinking of changing my job.' From the way Alex spoke, his children knew he was imparting a new and important fact. They said nothing. The fridge stopped whirring with a click.

'I need a move.'

'I thought you liked your job.'

'I do. I couldn't have a better job within the civil service structure. I suppose it's the civil service itself that gets me down. I am a bureaucrat, bound by the rules of my department.' He tapped his beer can with his finger. 'I can't help it, I'd like to teach again. It's my vocation.'

'But teaching made you ill. It was too much of a strain.'

'Looking back, Rod, I think it was a combination of circumstances, of which my teaching was a part, not a main cause. Don't look so worried, I'm not rushing into things. This is all at the theoretical stage. Come, let's go and sit in the garden.'

'OK.'

'It's much cooler out there now.'

They wrapped themselves up in the nearest supply of old coats and sat on the low wall at the edge of the lawn. Alex lit a cigar. He spoke in a low voice.

'The trouble is that my present job is full of hassle and low in fulfilment. When all the chat and admin are over, all I am is a middleman, a link man.'

'A patron too,' said Julia.

Alex shrugged. 'Only in a sense. Teaching may be hard and draining, but if you're good at it, it's one of the most rewarding of jobs.'

Julia knew that Alex was a brilliant teacher; the first time she had seen him in action, at an open seminar on Imperialism, when she and Rod had sat at the back to listen, she had found it difficult to see this incisive, inspiring man as the same person as her ordinary, often uncommunicative father. He had even looked slightly different; she had found the whole experience disturbing as well as impressive. She watched her father's cigar glow red in the dark as he drew on it, and wanted to say: it is bound to make you ill again, you do it so intensely. It isn't worth the price you'll pay. She could not bring the words out.

Alex took off his glasses and put them on the wall beside him so that he could rub his eyes. His weak eyesight often gave him headaches, and he had one now. 'Of course, I know it's taking the risk that I might crack up again. I'm sure that's what you're thinking. It's true, I might. It is a risk. But what's life without risks, without giving your real self even if it costs you dear.'

'I thought,' said Rod slowly, 'that one of the good things about your present job was its variety.'

A police car siren wailed in the distance.

'Variety of a sort. I meet a lot of different people, and see a wide range of "artistic endeavour", I agree. But I'm a parasite, a negotiator. I don't give of myself at all. My talents are unused. I've always thought it was a crime not to use the talents one is given. If you let them sleep you pay even more dearly in the end than you do for over-straining them.'

Rod fiddled with an empty snail shell. 'Well, when are you going back to teaching?' he asked after a silence.

'Not yet awhile. I'm in no hurry. It will take some time to find the ideal teaching job. But it's a comfort to have the prospect in view.' Alex yawned.

'What does Mum think?'

'I haven't told her yet. I don't really know why I've discussed it with you two now—I suppose our good evening has made me loquacious. Don't mention anything to Nell.' He yawned again. 'I'll break her in gently.' He saw the light still on upstairs in their bedroom. 'I don't know, I might tell her tonight, if she hasn't already gone to sleep.' He stood up. 'You two must go to bed. It's extremely late.'

'We'll go soon.'

'Very soon.' Alex kissed them both goodnight—it was a long while since he had last kissed Rod—and walked to the kitchen door. 'That was a good evening indeed.'

''Night Dad.'

In silence Rod and Julia sat watching the garden's hedgehog shuffle across the end of the lawn and disappear into a flowerbed. The murmur of voices came down from their parents' bedroom above them.

'What do you make of all that?' asked Julia quietly. She swung herself astride the wall; Rod did the same so that they were facing one another.

'Don't know. If Dad's really better, it's a good thing for him to go back to teaching if that's what he badly wants to do. He must

29

feel very secure in himself to consider a big change like this; perhaps the depressions really have gone for ever. After all, they started suddenly enough.'

'I don't think Mum's going to like the thought of him going back to teaching.'

'She won't have much choice if he's made up his mind. Dad never listens to anyone if he doesn't want to.' Laughter came down from another window, hastily smothered.

'Lucy and Betty are still awake, the little dears.'

'They are so boring. I can't see what Lucy sees in Betty.'

'Search me. Lucy herself is pretty awful at the moment. It's funny, but I really feel I have nothing whatever in common with her.'

'Why funny, Ju? People seem to expect brothers and sisters to get on with each other, but there's no reason why they should. Is there?'

'No.' They smiled at each other. At that moment a window swung wide open and Alex hissed: 'Go to bed, you two. It's well after one o'clock.'

'In a minute.'

'Now.'

Julia stood on the wall, her arms wide. 'No night may be as fine as this, no conversation so absorbing, no garden scents so heavy in the air,' she chanted.

'Ridiculous girl.'

'We'll go to bed soon, promise. Though I'm not a bit tired. Ten more minutes.'

'Only ten. Goodnight again.' The window was pulled in.

'Actually I'm beginning to feel sleepy.' Rod stretched and lay back on the wall behind him. There was a sound of glass crunching and cracking. 'Oh, God.' Rod rolled off the wall; there lay Alex's glasses, frame and lenses broken. 'Why on earth did the silly fool leave them out here.'

Julia picked them up. 'They've completely had it. How awful. But he's got another pair.'

'He hasn't any more. He was complaining the other day that he couldn't find his spare ones anywhere. I remember Nell saying she hadn't seen them for ages either. Hell. *Hell.*'

'Never mind Rod, it wasn't really your fault.'

Rod sat down again, all sleepiness gone. 'It'll upset him. He can't manage without them.'

'Perhaps the oculist can do a rushed job.'

'Let's hope so.' Rod picked up the snail shell and crushed it. 'Why didn't I break you instead.' They sat in a depressed silence.

'He can wear his prescription sunglasses.' Rod brightened. 'Of course. That's a comfort. At least he'll be able to see.' There was a pause, and then he added: 'I wonder if Alex said anything to Nell about changing his job.'

'Bet he didn't.'

'Probably not.' He lay back again on the wall. 'I've often wondered why Nell doesn't get a job of some sort. Not so much for the money as for something to do. I've often wondered what she does all day.'

'She seems perfectly happy running the house and us and the garden.'

'Yes, she seems it. But I wonder. I've never asked her, have you?'

'It sounds a bit silly to say: Mum, are you happy being a mother and a housewife?' Julia laughed. 'Besides, if she'd wanted a job she'd have got herself one.'

'But would she? She always puts us first, and doesn't believe in complaining. She doesn't talk much about her own feelings either. Perhaps at heart she feels frustrated and unfulfilled.'

'Oh go on, Rod. She doesn't look it to me.'

'I'm just pointing out that one can never be sure what another person feels.'

Julia gazed abstractedly at her parents' bedroom window and thought about the secrecy of people's lives. One accepted them at their face value, knowing at the same time that this could be very misleading. Very early in her life Julia had become aware that people said one thing and meant another; professed they acted in one way, and acted in another. When she was five, on the day she was leaving nursery school to go on to the 'big' school, she heard the headmistress say to Nell: 'I love children. Everything they do interests me.' Julia had stared at her owlishly and known without thinking that Miss Stanton did not like children greatly and at heart found their activities tedious, despite her superficial enthusiasm. Miss Stanton, fat Miss Stanton with her jolly, empty laugh; how odd she should remember her so well.

Impatiently, Julia turned to Rod. 'But surely Mum couldn't fool us all these years. Even if people don't actually say what they're feeling they can't help letting you sense it after a while.'

'Nell's a secretive person. Like me.' He sat up again, and their eyes met. 'You know me better than anyone, for instance, and yet there are many things about me you don't know.'

Julia swallowed. 'That sounds very ominous.' She tried to laugh. 'I suppose you find me an open book.'

'I do not. We're all full of surprises, however well we know each other.'

'Well, anyway, surely if Mum wanted to get herself a job she'd have done it.' Julia felt she had had enough of this disturbing discussion. She rearranged the coat over her shoulders as a sudden gust of wind rustled the mulberry tree.

'In many ways you're as like Alex as I'm like Nell. The other day I noticed specially how much you and he had in common—the day he got so angry about the Croxleys.'

'I suppose I have a lovely future of black depressions to look forward to.'

'Oh for heaven's sake, Ju, don't talk like that. And keep your voice down.'

But they had in fact touched on Julia's secret fear. She knew how like her father she was; she had nightmares about the implications. 'I don't look in the least bit like him.'

'No, not really. A bit about the eyes. But you get excited in the way he does, you switch off like he does and then blow hot again five minutes later. You have the same sort of drive—I can't really explain it.'

'Maybe I have.' Julia got up and walked over to the mulberry tree. 'I'm going to climb the tree.'

'You change the subject like he does too.' Rod followed her.

Julia laughed and took her long skirt off; she still had her bikini on underneath. 'I haven't climbed it for years.'

The first lap was a scramble but after that she disappeared upwards with ease.

'Don't be a fool and break any branches,' hissed Rod.

'Don't fuss. It's lovely up here.'

'Enjoy it. I'm going to bed.'

'Goodnight then.'

Rod hesitated by the wall, looking at the broken spectacles, then left them there and went into the kitchen. Julia sat on her high perch, ready to commune with nature. But her thigh hurt where she had scraped it, and she felt chilly. She tried in vain to find a comfortable position, and a fresh gust of wind made her shiver. It was no good; the magic evening was over.

3

Sunday dawned even hotter; dry, freak heat. The mess of un-washed dishes in the kitchen looked depressing in the bright sun-light. Nell, down first, stifled a sense of duty, made coffee and went outside. She stretched out in a deckchair and shut her eyes, letting the sun stream into her. Her slight hangover made her feel pleas-antly disembodied.

Then Julia came out accompanied by the sounds of a Schubert symphony; she put the transistor radio down on the patio wall and sat beside it. 'Oh Lord, Alex's glasses.'

'What about them?'

'He left them lying on the wall last night and Rod lay on them by accident. They're smashed to pieces.'

As this sank in Nell winced. 'Oh, no. He's lost his spare ones too.' Though she had not moved, her body was now tense.

Julia poured herself some coffee. 'Is he up yet?'

'No. I left him fast asleep.'

As if on cue, Alex leant out of the bedroom window, his face screwed up in the bright light.

'Anyone seen my glasses?'

Both Nell and Julia got to their feet. 'I'm afraid they're broken,' said Nell in apprehension. 'It seems Rod sat on them last night.'

'You left them on the wall, Dad—'

'*Broken*. How broken?'

Rod, in tattered pyjamas with top and bottom unmatching, came quickly out of the kitchen. 'I'm terribly sorry, Dad. I smashed them by accident—they were on the wall and I didn't see them. They've had it.'

Rage poured out of Alex. 'God damn it. I just can't manage without glasses.' He disappeared.

'You'd think I'd done it on purpose.'

'Please Rod, play it cool.' Nell rubbed her forehead distractedly. 'He'll be bad-tempered for days until he gets his new ones. Oh, why did you have to do it after such a good evening.'

'Oh, for heaven's sake, Mum.' Rod poured himself some coffee and walked away up the garden with it, a scarecrow figure.

Alex did not appear. After a while Lucy and Betty came out, dressed for the day. 'What's got into Dad? He's crashing about upstairs turning the study upside down. I asked him what was the matter and he just shouted at me.'

'He's looking for his spare glasses, I imagine. Rod broke his good ones.' Nell put down her half-drunk coffee and went inside to help him. The sight of the chaos in the kitchen made her turn back to snap : 'And you kids can do your bit by clearing up this ghastly mess.' She did not wait for a reply.

Betty looked nervous. 'Shall we do it now?' No one moved or answered her, so she sat down. She longed for cornflakes and bacon and egg but they did not seem to be forthcoming. Lucy yawned and day-dreamed.

Julia banged the paving stones savagely with her slipper. 'Why can't our family keep a good mood going for longer than a day? I came down feeling all was well with the world and now we're at loggerheads.' She threw her slipper up into the mulberry tree where it stuck fast. Lucy giggled. 'Come on, let's go and wash up.' Rod joined them and the work was swiftly done. As they finished the searchers arrived in the kitchen.

'No spare glasses?'

'No sign. We're now looking for Alex's prescription sunglasses.'

'With them at least I won't be completely blind.'

Alex's defenceless eyes were watering in the glare.

'They're in the car,' said Julia triumphantly. 'I remember seeing them in the dashboard pocket.'

'Of course.' Nell ran out with relief to fetch them. Alex put the glasses on and the whole family settled back in the garden. Julia made more toast and coffee, Lucy and Betty fried themselves eggs. The Sunday newspaper was divided up and silence reigned.

Only Nell did not read; she lay comatose, her skin bluish white in the sun. She was tired anyway, and the calming down of Alex had exhausted her. 'I meant to go to church this morning,' she murmured. 'It's too late now. Perhaps I'll go this evening instead.' No one commented, and after another pause Nell heaved herself up and went inside. She saw the broken glasses on the kitchen table and threw them firmly into the garbage-bin.

Julia started to turn over on her daybed and it jack-knifed, throwing her off. 'Unfeeling brute. Something's wrong with this wretched thing.' She straightened it out and tried to sit on it, and it did the same again. She swore.

'Do keep still, Julia. You're disturbing the peace.'

'Sorry, Dad.' Over his head, she met Rod's expressive glance. She left the daybed on its side and said: 'Let's go for a swim.' There was a Lido in the nearest park.

'Everyone will be there on a day like this.' Rod was unenthusiastic.

'So what,' said Lucy, who was varnishing her toenails a curious brown colour. 'I like it when it's full.'

'I don't. The answer, Ju, is to go much later just before it closes. That's the best time.'

'All right, let's do that. The pool will have warmed up in the sun by then.' Julia shook her head. 'Mind you, in my present condition I think I'd sink.'

'I might come with you,' said Alex.

'Fine.' Julia spoke quickly to cover her disappointment. She and Rod specially enjoyed their amiable swims. When Alex was there he nagged them to do high dives which they happened to be good at, and liked to see them race each other. He was proud of their agility in the water, being a poor swimmer himself. His presence, though, took the relaxed fun out of their swims; in turn, they were obstinate and dived and showed off less than they might have. 'Fine,' Julia repeated, and went inside to get dressed.

'Don't go overboard with enthusiasm,' Alex called after her. She ignored it. Lucy and Betty followed her in, deciding as they did so to swim on Betty's way home. Lucy was wearing a dress that had been Julia's; on Lucy it was delightful.

'I always looked a mess in that dress. How do you do it, you horrible girl,' growled Julia as she went upstairs.

'I changed the belt, and always wear this scarf with it.'

'I hate you.'

Lucy grinned, and went on her way with Betty.

Alex developed a bad migraine, which he said was due to wearing dark glasses. He sat reading in suffering silence, and his mood cast a blight on them all.

'Why don't you have a sleep?' Nell suggested after a lunch during which the family were as low as they had been elated the night before. 'Give your eyes a rest.'

'I've got work to do.' He went up to his study and remained there for the rest of the afternoon to the relief of the others.

'I must get that oculist to make him new glasses with express speed,' said Nell with feeling.

When, later, Rod and Julia got themselves ready to go swimming, Nell reminded them that Alex had wanted to join them. She then left the house on her own to go to Evensong. Rod shouted up the stairs. 'Come on, Dad, we're off to the pool now.'

'What?'

'You said you wanted to come swimming.'

Alex came slowly downstairs, his dark glasses looking wholly out of place inside. 'I'd forgotten you were going. Won't the pool be closed by now?'

'It stays open until seven.'

'I'm tempted to come, but I don't think I will. My headache is so appalling.'

'It might do your headache good,' said Rod. Julia was already at the door, eager to go and wash the day's heat away.

'No, I think I won't come in fact.'

'Please yourself.' Julia did not mean to sound so offhand; nor did she mean to slam the front door, but she did that too.

The pool was unusually warm after two hot days, and almost empty now. The sun was low enough to filter through the trees in the surrounding park, making broken lights on the water. Rod and Julia lazed, dived, swam, lazed again, hardly talking, luxuriating in the beauty of water and late sunlight. Eventually they were asked to leave the pool by the attendant, who had been brushing and sluicing round the pool for some time. He leant on his brush smiling at them as they climbed out.

'Always the best time, this.' His T-shirt had a bosomy girl printed on it, at odds with the kind careworn face above.

'Isn't it perfect.'

'Mind you, seven o'clock on a fine morning is almost as good. Very bright and shiny. There's a chap, a solicitor, comes here every morning slap on ten past seven. Out by half past. Like clockwork.'

'Even on wet days?'

'Rain or shine, May till September.'

Rod and Julia stood and talked to him until they were shivering. As they wandered home, refreshed and peaceful, they met Nell returning from church. They saw her before she saw them and were struck by her bent, sad air. She smiled brilliantly when she saw them, and ran across the road to join them. As they strolled past a pub, Rod said:

'Come on, Mum, let's stop here for a drink.'

Rod tipped out the loose change in his pocket. 'I've got enough for a beer or shandy each. Sit down and I'll bring it out to you. Come on, sit.' Rod led her to a wooden bench and pushed her gently down.

'I ought to get home.'

'Why? Give me one good reason.'

Nell laughed. 'Can't think of any. All right, I'll have a cider.' She watched her son go through the pub door with a half-proud, half-desolate expression on her face.

Julia was busy pushing her wet hair into shape as she said with a sigh: 'That was a smashing swim.'

'I thought Alex was going with you. Has he already gone home?'

'He didn't come; he changed his mind because his headache was so bad.'

'I'm not surprised. I'm glad, actually—he always gets such inflamed eyes from chlorinated water. That on top of eye-strain would have been too much.' She grinned ruefully.

Julia turned her collar right down. 'I must get my hair cut. My collar gets soaked with my hair this length. Perhaps I'll have it cut very short.'

'You're always saying that. It would suit you to have a short gamine sort of style.'

'The trouble is, when it comes to the point it's such a jump to go from long hair to short hair.'

'Where's Lucy, by the way?'

'Where do you think.'

'She's a funny child. Ever since she was tiny she has always had one bosom friend to the exclusion of all others. You've never really had close friends until the Croxleys came along.'

'I know. I miss them.'

Rod came out of the pub with a beer, a cider and a shandy. They sat in silence for a while, watching the children in an adjacent playground.

'By the way, what did you think of Alex changing his job? I know he told you.'

Rod drank down inches of his beer. 'Yes, last night in the garden. I don't know, Mum. What do you?'

'I'm absolutely against a change at the moment.'

'Why? He had very good reasons for changing.'

'I know, Julia. I think it's premature. He's got a job that's interesting and full of variety and at least it doesn't overtax him. Later on he could go back to teaching.'

'What did Dad say?'

'Of course I didn't tell him I was so against it; I just said I understood why he wanted to change. I did say I thought it was a bit soon.'

'But what was his reaction?'

'He was disappointed.'

'I bet he was more than disappointed.' Julia stared at her mother. 'He must have been very upset you didn't think his plan was a good one. Honestly, Mum, you underplay everything; when something's fantastic you say it's quite nice. It's the most maddening habit.'

'Don't go on at me, Julia. He didn't seem very upset or annoyed. I wasn't emphatic; we just discussed it lightly.' Nell examined her cider, her expression shut.

'He hasn't had one of his bouts for so long perhaps it's safe now to go back to teaching. He seemed sure he could cope. He's just a nice normal neurotic like the rest of us, so he probably could,' said Rod.

They laughed. Nell said: 'He is well now, I agree; but that's why I don't want him to go back to teaching.'

'But Mum, if he's doing a job that doesn't fulfil him—that's how he described it to Julia and me—won't that make him feel frustrated in the long run and trigger off other problems?'

'His present job suits him well and he does it well.'

'If he *needs* to change—' began Julia.

'Look.' Nell was annoyed. 'I've been married to Alex for twenty years and I know him by now. He's always been someone who liked change for change's sake, so I take that with a pinch of salt. Other fields are much greener than his own, and that's something no one will alter. The idea of going back to teaching isn't new; he's a good teacher and he loves it—'

'He says it's his vocation—'

'But he knows in his heart it's too draining emotionally and physically for him, because he does it at such a white hot level. He'll drop the idea of his own accord, you'll see.'

Julia and Rod sat in silence, uneasy but unable to answer her.

'So let's change the subject. And actually, I ought to go, or none of us will get any food tonight.' She stood up. 'But there's no hurry for you to come now if you don't want to.'

'No, we'll come.' They walked the short distance home in silence, each busy with their thoughts. Nell felt in her handbag for the front door key.

'Oh dear, I came out without a key.'

'We haven't got one either.' Julia rang the bell and noticed that the paint on the door had begun to bubble in the sun; she was about to press her nail into one of the bubbles when Nell stopped her. 'Don't you dare. Ring again harder. He may be in the garden.'

'Don't say he's gone out.'

Julia rang long and loud, but in vain. Nell searched through her handbag again, and then examined the bay windows. They were all closed because no one had used those rooms during the day.

'He's probably gone out for a walk. It's such a lovely evening.'

'Probably.'

They gazed at the front of the house, looking for a place to enter. But the Parrishes had been burgled not so long before, and the house was now very secure. There were windows open on the top floor, but no means of getting there. A household ladder would not begin to reach.

'I could break a window.' Rod looked round for a suitable object to do it with.

'Try ringing the bell just once more. After all, Alex may just have fallen asleep somewhere and if we persevere we might wake him.' Nell spoke lightly, but a cloud had descended on the three of them, and they did not meet each other's eyes. Julia rang again.

'Of course, we could wait until he comes back. Wherever he is, he won't be that long, surely.' Julia went to the gate and looked up and down the road. 'Let's go back to the pub and have another drink rather than hang about here.'

'What about Lucy—she might come back and wonder where we all are.'

'We could leave a note on the door telling them both where we are. Got anything to write on, Mum?'

Nell made a pretence of looking through her bag, but her hands were shaking. She looked up and met Rod's eyes; the dread in them was almost palpable. Julia came back from the pavement.

'No sign of him.'

'Break a window, Rod will you.' Nell tried to laugh. 'I know it's a little dramatic, but I don't want to wait out here any longer.

When Alex sees the broken window he'll be very annoyed, but there we are.'

'Breaking glass seems to be my rôle this weekend,' murmured Rod, as he wrapped a towel round a piece of brick edging and broke a lower sash window, carefully clearing the entire pane of glass before he climbed in. He went through and opened the front door. As the three of them walked in, the sound of the radio came faintly from the garden. They smiled with relief at each other.

'There—he was in the garden all the time and the music must have drowned the bell. We must get a louder bell fitted, it's uselessly soft anyway.' Nell went straight upstairs to change her decent shoes for sandals.

'Well, come on. Let's go and find the old devil and tell him the good news about the window.'

Rod led the way down to the kitchen; their cat was sitting on the draining board, miaowing. Julia shoved it off as she filled a kettle. The music came loudly now from the patio, and they could see the top of Alex's head in a deckchair. Julia put the kettle on and leant against the Aga, chilly after her long swim. Rod joined her.

'I think I'll let Nell tell him about the window.'

'Coward.'

There was something about the way Alex's arm hung down beside his chair which caught Rod's eye and made him frown. Julia followed his gaze, and then grabbed his arm. Neither of them moved. They could hear Nell walking about upstairs, humming. The radio music stopped and an announcer's voice burbled. A sparrow hopped past Alex's chair picking up crumbs. It flew off as Rod suddenly walked out of the kitchen.

'Dad, wake up. We're all back.' Rod's hand went out to shake Alex's shoulder when he froze, his eyes fixed in horror on Alex's face. Julia had followed him to the kitchen door, and she whimpered: 'What is it? What is it?'

'Shut up.'

She watched while Rod picked up Alex's hand to feel his pulse, and touched his forehead.

'*Mum. Mum.*' Rod's shout was a hoarse screech. 'Get an ambulance. Oh God. Quick.' Nell came to the bedroom window, her hand pressed to the side of her face. It seemed to Rod that she stood there for ever.

'Get an ambulance.' He knocked Alex's glass over as he rushed towards the kitchen door, pushing Julia out of the way. She started to whimper again. Nell pushed past her too; she seemed unable to get out of the way. Nell stood in front of Alex, her hand still up against her face as if she had an unbearable toothache. She did not touch him. After a few seconds she walked back to the kitchen and went to the telephone. Rod had already dialled 999 and asked for an ambulance. Still seemingly calm, she took the receiver from him and dialled Doctor Railton's number. The ringing tone went on and on. A fine summer Sunday evening and they were all out.

'He's not there,' she whispered. But she kept the receiver near her ear, numb, and then with a clatter the phone was answered.

'Hullo,' panted a child's voice.

'Doctor Railton. I must speak to him.'

'He's putting the car away. We've just got back from—'

'Get him now. Please.' There was a long pause. Nell stood white and calm, her fingers twisting and re-twisting the cord. Rod stood behind her.

The child's voice came again. 'Dad says who is it please, can he ring you back—'

'No, no. It's Nell Parrish. *Get him now.*' She almost screamed at the poor child, who from the clatter dropped the receiver on the floor. At last Doctor Railton's voice came on the line.

'Mrs Parrish. What can I do for you?'

'It's Alex. He—he—' Then she seemed to go into a trance. Rod took the receiver from her cold hand.

'It's Rod, Doctor Railton. My father's in a coma.' Rod's voice shook. 'I tried to feel his pulse. I—I'm not very good at it. Yes, sir. Just now, a few minutes ago; we've all been out for a couple of hours. Yes. We don't know what he took. Yes. Thank you.' He put down the receiver. 'He's coming immediately. He says the short time we were out is a good thing—'

Rod gazed at his mother, and felt numb, as if most of his brain and body were anaesthetized. The whole situation was so unreal that if his father had walked in and said 'Fooled you', he would have felt neither surprise nor relief. Feeling was dead in him.

Nell suddenly ran down the corridor through the kitchen and back to Alex. She grabbed his shoulders, kneeling in front of him, then took his face between her hands, turning it from side to side. She spoke distractedly to him, tears pouring down her face : 'Alex, Alex, you fool. You've done it, at last you've done it, you fool, you fool—' Her foot made his glass roll; beside it lay his dark glasses. He reeked of whisky as if he had spilt some down his front. Her face fell forward into his lap and she sobbed aloud.

Julia sat on the stairs, unable to move. Both she and Rod could hear Nell in the garden. Rod walked aimlessly yet tensely into the kitchen, and hovered. He noticed as he tapped his fingers obsessively that there was a small aspirin bottle lying empty in the sink. Rod had had an aspirin from the self-same bottle that morning and knew that of the 100 announced on the label, at least 50 had still been in it. He picked the bottle up, put it down, picked it up again. He wanted to show it to Nell, but could not. He stood in the kitchen door blankly, with the bottle in his hand, and a voice high up in his brain repeated : 'Please come, ambulance. Please come, ambulance,' endlessly.

Julia came up behind him and he held up the bottle.

'They'll pump him out,' she said. 'Like they pumped me out when I swallowed that disinfectant when I was small. I'm sure it'll be all right.'

Rod did not seem to register what she said. She went back to the hall, waiting for the door-bell. Even so, she jumped when it rang explosively. There was Doctor Railton.

'Where is he?'

'In the garden.'

'The ambulance should be here by now.' Doctor Railton ran through the house, and as he did so there was another ring at the door and Julia let in the ambulance men. She sat down on the stairs. She was afraid of seeing Alex's face. But she had no chance

44

to, because the ambulance men bulked so large as they carried him through on a stretcher that his face was obscured by their backs. Doctor Railton came past with Nell and Rod; he held the aspirin bottle up as he said:

'You're certain this was only half-full?'

'Absolutely.'

'There's every hope. As long as he didn't take anything else. Have you any poisonous substances or other pills, sleeping tablets, barbiturates?'

'We only have about four or five sleeping tablets upstairs as a standby—very mild ones—and no barbiturates. I have a bottle of ammonia up in the bathroom—'

'Run and see, Julia.' Julia brought the bottle down; it was almost full and clearly had not been touched.

'Thank goodness. I shouldn't worry; it looks as if he took all the aspirin with some whisky, but only that, and with aspirin the dangerous period begins after four hours. We've caught him soon enough. There's every hope.' He smiled at the Parrishes, then put his arm round Nell's shoulders. 'Now I'm going to the hospital with your mother, and she needs you to stay here and mind the fort.'

'I'll ring you, darlings.' Nell was white. 'Be careful how you tell Lucy.' She grabbed her handbag, and they were gone.

Julia, still sitting on the stairs, leant back against the wall and closed her eyes. Rod sat down on a lower stair, and there was a long silence in the house. The curtain flapped at the broken window in the sitting-room, and the wet bathing things lay piled unnoticed on the window-sill outside. A gust of hot wind through the house blew papers off the hall table, and these fluttered to the floor and lay there unregarded. The hall clock ticked loudly; Julia found herself concentrating her mind on the tick-TACK, tick-TACK. Her brain pulsed with the sound, unable to cope with thought.

Rod went into the kitchen, and came back with two bananas; he offered her one, but she shook her head. She could not have

45

swallowed anything. He ate them both, and then went and stretched out on the sofa. Julia stayed where she was on the stairs, her eyes shut again.

Twenty minutes later the telephone jarred through the silence. It was Nell, though not with news.

'I felt dreadful leaving you both like that. Are you all right?' She sounded cheerful.

'Yes, we're fine. Lucy isn't back yet.' Julia tried to sound cheerful too : 'What's the news?'

'No news yet. Doctor Railton says there really is every hope; the only danger lies not in the aspirin itself, which hasn't been there long enough, but in pumping out the stomach of someone in a coma.'

'Which hospital are you at?'

'St Jude's General. I'll ring you again soon. Let's hope Lucy will be back by then.'

As the pips went and Nell rang off there was Lucy at the front door. She pushed the bell and peered through the letterbox as she did so.

'Hurry. I'm dying to go to the loo.' She rushed past Rod upstairs. When she came down again, she went on : 'Why is the window broken? Have we had another burglary or something?' She frowned when she saw Rod's face. 'What's the matter? What's happened?'

'Dad's been rushed off to hospital. They think he'll be all right, but he took an overdose.'

Lucy gazed at him blankly while the implications of this began to sink in. 'An overdose . . .' She sounded puzzled.

'Of aspirins.'

'But why?'

'Don't be so stupid, Lucy. People take overdoses to kill themselves, that's why.' His tone was savage, and his lips started to quiver. He rushed past Lucy up the stairs and banged the door of his room. Lucy looked frightened.

'What's happened, Ju? Please tell me what's happened.' Julia sat down on the stairs again, and Lucy sat down beside her. 'We

46

came back with Mum after our swim and found Dad unconscious.' She paused, remembering the sight of her father's limp arm and hand. 'Then Doctor Railton came and the ambulance and they all went off with Mum as well to St Jude's Hospital. She's just tele-phoned to say Dad's bound to be all right; the aspirin hasn't been inside him long enough to hurt him.'

Lucy listened to this explanation, frowning. Because she had not been close to the moments of horror, she could ask the question no one wanted asked : 'But why on earth should Dad try to kill him-self?'

Julia put her hands over her face. 'God knows.' She hated the question to be asked so baldly; in her mind, echoing clearly, was her offhand coldness and the door she had banged in her father's face when she left to go swimming.

The telephone rang. Julia leapt at it. The warm voice of Connie Parrish, her grandmother, filled her ear. 'Hallo, darling. Isn't this weather amazing? I've just spent the most beautiful day in the garden doing nothing and loving it. What have you all been doing, my love?'

'Oh Granny—' wailed Julia and started to cry.

'What on earth's the matter?'

'Oh Granny, Dad's taken an overdose and they've rushed him to hospital.'

'Dear God. When?'

'Just now. I mean, it's all happened since teatime. Mum's gone to the hospital with the ambulance and we're just waiting for news.'

'What did he take?'

'Aspirin. Doctor Railton says there's every hope.'

'I'll come straight up. I'll be with you in two hours. You poor darlings.'

'Mum rang to say they're pumping him out now.'

'I'm sure everything will be all right and he'll be fine in a day or two.'

Although she knew her grandmother always took an over-optimistic view of life, Julia was comforted.

'I'll leave as soon as I've organized myself and arranged for someone to feed the cats. See you very soon.'

Rod's head came over the landing bannister rail as Julia put the receiver down. 'Who was that?'

'Granny. She's coming here as soon as she can. Isn't that marvellous?'

'Did you tell her?'

'Of course I told her. That's why she's coming. Oh, how lovely. Dear Granny—she's just what we need.'

Rod gazed at her sombrely, and went back to his room. Lucy switched the television on, but Julia found she could not watch it. Time crept by, and there was no telephone call from Nell. Finally Julia went into Rod's room and said: 'Do you think something is wrong?'

Rod was lying on his bed gazing at the ceiling; a book lay face downwards on the bed beside him. 'Why?'

'Mum hasn't rung yet.'

'Everything moves at a snail's pace in a hospital.'

'All the same, don't you feel that by now—'

'I don't feel anything.'

This appeared to be so true that Julia stood there with nothing to say. Rod's room was in its usual chaos—every surface was covered with objects and most of the floor with gear of various sorts. His work table held tottering piles of books and files. Once every so often Nell made him have a blitz, but in between chaos built up as before. Drawers hung open, cupboard doors gaped; even the pictures were askew, with the odd tie hung on the corners.

'A bigger tornado than usual has hit this room.'

'I like it. This is the way I'm comfortable.' Rod picked his book up.

'I couldn't stand it.' Julia left the room, in her heart admiring the sheer splendour of the mess, and Rod for his ease in it. She went to her own room and lay on her bed too, waiting blankly for time to pass.

The front door opened and Nell's voice called them. All three rushed to the hall. They could see by her face that the news was good.

'I'm sorry I didn't ring you but all the telephone boxes were either in use or out of order, so rather than lose time I took a taxi and came straight home.' She smiled. 'Alex is all right now, and came round for a while though I didn't see him. He's fast asleep now.' Her smile was bright, too bright. 'Now, what about some food. I suddenly feel ravenous.' As they followed her to the kitchen they all knew why their sense of relief was shadowed—by the horror that Alex should have tried to kill himself at all.

'I need a drink.' Nell sighed as she looked through the bottles in the larder; she and Alex did not drink as a regular habit and there was rarely much in the house. She avoided the remnant of the whisky and poured herself some brandy from a quarter bottle bought the previous Christmas.

'Oh, Mum, Granny's coming. She should be here any minute.'

'Oh *no*.' Nell's reaction startled Julia. 'Why did you have to tell her?'

'She just happened to ring up, Mum. I couldn't help telling her, I was so upset—' Tears started to flow, and she slumped down at the kitchen table and put her face in her hands. 'I thought, I thought,' she gulped, 'you'd be pleased to see Granny—'

'My poor love. Of course I am really.' Nell put her arm round Julia's shoulders. 'It's just that Granny does so hate things not to be happy and bright, and I don't think I could bear to be told to look on the cheerful side of life at the moment.'

'There isn't a cheerful side,' said Rod flatly, 'so Granny will have to lump it.' He watched his mother sip her brandy. Her forehead was covered in sweat; the kitchen was stiflingly hot despite the fact that every window was open.

'There is, Rod.' Julia's voice was muffled but she had stopped crying. 'Dad didn't die.'

All four of them were silent; wan and exhausted as they were, nothing could lift their hearts. The relief that Alex was alive had passed; they now had to live with what had happened.

'I wish we had a fan in the kitchen,' said Lucy fretfully.

'You keep saying that.'

'Well, in this hot weather we need it.'

Rod turned impatiently to his mother. 'Tell us what happened at the hospital then.' Nell with her usual reserve had as yet told them nothing.

'I spent most of the time in the corridor.'

'Did you speak to Dad afterwards?'

'No, Rod. He wasn't in a fit state to talk. They said I could see him tomorrow.' Nell fiddled with the ice tray, trying to loosen more cubes to put in her drink. 'We can all go and see him tomorrow. He's in a big ward, by the way.'

'With lots of other people?' Julia was slightly appalled.

'The ward seemed full.'

'Dad will hate it.'

'He might not.' Nell did not sound hopeful.

'Since family life drove him to suicide perhaps being in an anonymous ward with a lot of strangers will suit him fine,' said Rod bitterly.

'*Rod*. Don't be ridiculous.' Nell's face was red. At that moment the doorbell rang; it was Connie Parrish, full of kisses. Her long white hair was in a rather less tidy chignon than usual.

'My darlings. Nell. I can see by your face all is well.' Having kissed them all, she handed over her usual basket of fresh eggs and vegetables to Nell. 'I'm sorry there aren't more strawberries, but this simply hasn't been a good year at all.' She bustled into the sitting-room and sat down. The family trailed after her.

'Lucy, I know your birthday isn't for ten days or so, but I had your present ready so I've brought it with me. It's not the sort of thing one can post.' She smiled mysteriously and handed her car keys to Lucy. 'Go and fetch it; it's in the back of the car. I left it there because I wasn't sure whether now would be a good moment to give it to you. But I think it is, don't you?'

'Oh *yes*. How exciting.' Lucy ran out and came back starry-eyed. 'Look what I've got.' She held a small, beautifully ornate Victorian birdcage. It was freshly painted white, with curlicues of red and blue. Inside was a small stuffed canary, its glass eyes gleaming. They all crowded round the cage.

'The key's on the side. Wind it up.' Connie Parrish watched Lucy as she carefully wound it. 'Now release that catch.' The bird whirred into life, singing lustily and moving its head from side to side. Peals of realistic song filled the room.

'Isn't it lovely? Oh, Granny, you are wonderful.' Lucy flung her arms round her grandmother. Nell came in from the kitchen drawn by the bird's song.

'Connie, you shouldn't. It's a museum piece.'

'It's not, it's a present for all of you to enjoy. And don't think I paid the earth for it because I didn't—you know my friend in the village who's a dealer, well he got it for me in very bad condition and I did it up. The bird didn't work, but the watchmaker in the High Street put a new spring in for me and cleaned the mechanism, and here it is, working perfectly.'

The bird stopped in mid-tweet. Rod wound it up again, and off it went. Nell laughed.

'Oh, Connie, it's very you.'

'I think it's beautiful,' said Lucy. 'I adore it.'

'I must say I rather love it too.' Connie stood back, pleased with her canary's effect.

'You're jolly lucky, Lucy. It's an heirloom. You'll have to keep your friends' fiddling fingers off it.' Julia swallowed.

Connie put her arms round Julia's shoulders. 'Yes, it mustn't be over-wound. Or indeed, wound up too often.' She led Julia away towards the kitchen. 'Are you feeling better now, my sweet?'

'Yes and no.'

'Now that we're on our own, Nell, tell me exactly what happened.' Connie lay back on the sofa looking very tired, her hair messy and her shoes off. 'I couldn't go to bed without talking to you first.'

Nell described everything in, for her, unusual detail. Connie never interrupted. There was a long silence after Nell finished speaking; in fact she thought Connie had gone to sleep. She was just about to get up when Connie said: 'As I drove up here of course I thought all those endless useless thoughts: did I fail him as a child, where did I go wrong; etcetera, etcetera. Pointless questions, because one cannot know.'

'I don't think they're pointless.' Nell's voice was very quiet. 'Because we as a family obviously have failed him somehow.'

'Perhaps. Perhaps not. The failing could be all in him. Perhaps he can't use the love his normal loving family give him. You give him all you can.'

'But do we? Do we?'

'I think you do. It's his problem, his fault, if it doesn't satisfy him. He's a demanding person, and not always a giving person. He's been like that all his life. But he's very like his father; Tom used to rage about our lack of sympathy and interest in his doings, and it never seemed to occur to him that he hardly ever showed sympathy or interest in ours.'

'Alex isn't self-centred like that. He can be possessively interested. His interest isn't always very loving, perhaps.' Nell lay back, frowning. There was a long silence as each woman thought of the Alex she knew so intimately and yet so incompletely.

Nell broke the silence. 'Connie, has he ever tried, before I knew him, to commit suicide?'

'No. Not really.'

'What do you mean, not really?'

'Well, there was a teenage episode I can't regard as important. I remember unpacking his trunk after he had spent six months in France and I found several bottles of aspirin in a paper bag. I tackled him about them and he laughed. He said, I remember it so well, that he'd been absolutely miserable at one point because of loneliness, dislike of the place, and lack of ability to communicate with the girl of the house whom he rather fancied, and he'd bought the aspirins in a fit of despair. He said he'd hidden them in his trunk and never thought of them again, and I believed him. I think the girl began to return his interest and life looked up.' She stopped. Nell got the feeling she had more to say, but her mother-in-law went silent. Then a creak behind them startled them. Julia stood in the doorway.

'I'm sorry I made you jump, but I came down because I couldn't sleep.'

'I'm not surprised.' Nell patted the sofa beside her, but Julia sat down on the arm of a chair.

'It all keeps going round and round in my brain.'

'And in ours.' Connie looked exhausted.

'Mum, do you think he'd planned to do it all in advance?'

'Ah no. Doctor Railton said it had all the signs of a sudden decision, triggered off by events. Darling, if he had planned it, he would have been more efficient.'

Julia considered this with mixed feelings.

'Something tipped the scales.'

'A whole series of small things probably. But he wasn't organized, Ju. Whatever made him do it was not arrived at rationally.'

'He didn't sit down coldly and work it out.'

'No, I'm sure he didn't. Think of his mood last night.'

'It's one of the things I can't get out of my mind. We were all so happy.'

'Doctor Railton said that suicide attempts are often a cry for help; the person doing it subconsciously hopes he won't succeed.'

'It's rather an extreme way of asking for help, particularly from someone like Dad.'

'I know, Ju, I know.'

The curtains billowed in the broken window, the fabric rubbing on the bare wood frame.

'Give him time,' said Connie slowly, 'and he'll probably tell us himself.' She got up and stretched, and began feeling with her feet for her shoes.

'I think it was me who tipped the scales.'

It took a few moments for Nell and Connie to register what Julia had said. 'What do you mean, you?'

'I was so horrid to him.'

'When?'

'When we were going swimming. First he said he'd come. That annoyed me for a start, and I expect I showed it. Then he decided not to, and though I didn't mean to, I slammed the front door in his face. I was cold and rude to him. I've been lying in bed thinking about it.'

'You've worked yourself up into a state about nothing at all,' said Connie unsympathetically. 'I'm sure a little thing like that wouldn't have had any appreciable effect.'

'But Granny—'

'No, Julia, we're all to blame, if any one of us is. I've been wondering whether it's my fault: after all, I brought him up. But I gave him all I had in the way of love and attention, and being an only child he didn't have to share it with anyone. What more could I have done?' There was a silence. Julia's thoughts were still with her own sense of guilt, but Nell found herself crying inwardly: much less, much less—you smothered him with it all. She shut her eyes and heard Connie go on: 'But we mustn't be morbid, we must stop worrying and wait for things to get back to normal and I'm sure in due course we'll learn why Alex did it.' Connie stifled a yawn. 'I must go to bed, it's after midnight. I'm never up after ten as a rule.' She got up and moved towards the door, hobbling a little with stiffness. 'He will tell us, you know. If he doesn't we'll ask him.'

'Goodnight, Connie.' Nell watched her go. Connie always made things sound too easy. Her attitude was that if you did not dwell upon the darker aspects of life, they went away. She did not sweep problems under carpets; she simply denied their existence. Nell sighed. Well, perhaps it would be easy. Alex would tell them. Nell knew, though, that it was always much more difficult to get the truth out of people than you envisaged. You could see yourself in your imagination saying: 'Tell me the truth, tell me what you really felt at the time'; yet in reality, faced by the person in question with all his emotions and thoughts, you would probably never even reach the right moment at which words like 'Tell me the truth' could be said, let alone get an answer which reflected even a part of the truth. Nell sighed again. Yet her children found it much easier than she did to talk about inner things, so perhaps they would be able to talk to Alex in a way she could not. She got up.

54

'I'm going to bed too. Come on, Julia, you must get some sleep. You were very late last night as well.'

'I'll just have a glass of milk first.' She kissed her mother and her grandmother goodnight and stood sipping her milk in the dark kitchen, staring out at the moonlit garden. The chairs were still out on the patio, in the disarray left by the removal of Alex. His chair was on its side.

Julia went outside and put it straight. The sky was clear and starlit above her; it would obviously be fine again tomorrow. She sat down on the low wall, aware that she was very tired but unable to find the energy to go upstairs. The cat rubbed itself against her leg. 'What did you see, you bad cat? I bet you watched him begin to die and just purred and closed your eyes. I wouldn't put it past you to have got on his lap when he was—he was—' Tears suddenly poured down her face. She tried to cuddle the cat for comfort, but it objected and escaped down the garden. Wearily, Julia made herself go in to bed.

4

The Parrishes' house the next morning had an atmosphere of bank holiday. No one got up to go to school; the house was silent, except for the flop of newspaper and post, until the doorbell rang at nine. It was Josie Chapman, who for years had 'done' for the Parrishes.

'Night on the tiles?' Josie gazed in surprise at Nell; it was unlike her still to be in a dressing-gown.

'Not really—though we were a bit late, I suppose. Everyone's overslept—the children are still in bed.'

'They'll be in trouble. Who's broke your window? And these were outside.' She held up the rolls of swimming things.

'Wasn't it stupid of us—we locked ourselves out. Rod had to break a window. We must get it mended today.' Nell prattled, wondering how they were going to keep what had happened secret. For Alex's sake, it would be best no one knew. She must ring his office at ten and make apologies. 'I'll go and wake everyone up.'

Josie watched her hurry up the stairs; things were not quite right and she was puzzled. She hung the wet towels and bathing suits in front of the Aga.

Nell went into each room in turn, and found everyone awake but still in bed. She warned them all to say nothing to Josie; Julia and Rod made no reply, though Julia nodded; Lucy, the unreliable one who found it impossible to keep a secret, said : 'Of course not, Mum. I won't breathe a word to anyone.'

The family descended for breakfast glumly.

'No one would mistake any of you for a ray of sunshine,' said Josie. She clattered round them while they slowly made breakfast. 'Don't mind me,' she said when Rod accidentally trod on her toe, 'I only come here for the fun. Well, come on, what's got into you all? Or have your schools thrown the lot of you out?' She said this to Rod, who was her favourite; she enjoyed verbal sparring with him.

But he just yawned, and said : 'We all felt rotten yesterday. Some bug or other. Headaches, the lot.'

Josie snorted. 'Your dad's managed to get himself to work all the same, I see. Or perhaps he didn't catch the plague.' Josie, who was never ill, had no patience whatever with sickness.

'That's right,' Rod said without fully meeting her eye.

'You don't look your usual beautiful self, I'll admit.' Josie began to fill a bucket with water. At that moment Connie appeared. 'Well, good morning, Mrs Parrish. This house is full of surprises this morning. Didn't know you were coming. Nice to see you.'

'It was rather a last-minute decision.' She smiled warmly, to cover her complete exhaustion. She had hardly slept at all. 'How are you, Josie dear?'

'Same as usual.' Josie's hold on life was so firm, and her good humour so deep, that they all knew what she meant. 'Even though a car tried to kill me on the way here. Ran up the pavement, inches from me feet. It was a really nasty moment.'

'Poor Josie. I bet you gave the driver an earful.'

'I did too.' She reflected on this. 'He didn't like it much. Honestly, these days you're courting death if you step outside the front door. I'll start on the sitting-room. It's pointless trying to do anything in here.' She clanked away with the vacuum cleaner, and set it going with a distant roar.

'Won't Josie find out anyway, with Dad in hospital?' Rod did not like having secrets from Josie. 'She's so canny.'

'We'll have to think of something. I'm sure he wouldn't like people to know—' Nell tailed off.

'You mean *you* don't want people to know.'

'Of course she doesn't,' said Connie. 'Have a little tact, Rod. It'll only make it more difficult for Nell if she has to deal with people's sympathy and also their curiosity.'

'I hadn't thought of that.'

Connie took some cold toast. 'Luckily life has a way of getting back to normal in spite of us. Thank God. Is this some of your mulberry jam, Nell?'

'Last year's.'

'I'll have some. It's so delicious.'

Visiting hours were in the early afternoon; St Jude's General was an old-fashioned hospital and strict about people coming in at other times. When breakfast was over the morning stretched emptily before the Parrishes. They felt flat and dispirited. Josie watched the family and wondered what had happened; for once she did not feel like asking.

'This is crazy,' said Rod to Julia, who was sitting aimlessly in his room. 'We should have gone to school. It just makes things worse, hanging about at home.'

'I absolutely agree. And I'm sure Dad doesn't want to see the lot of us. Mum and Granny would be quite enough.'

Rod sat at his desk tipping his chair back. 'I can't work at home in this atmosphere. Besides, I mustn't miss the experiments we're doing this afternoon.'

'Come on, let's go to school then.'

'Right.' Rod started to throw books into his large canvas hold-all.

Lucy refused to come with them. They sought out Nell to tell her they were going. She looked hard at both of them.

'Well, as you please. Though I'm sure Alex would be very pleased to see you.'

Rod kicked at his bag of books. 'I don't think I could stand going to the hospital,' he said, and picking up his bag, hurried from the house. Nell looked stricken, and Julia did not know what to do. She hovered miserably.

Connie rescued her.

'Nell, dear, it's much better they go to school if they feel like it. You and I will go to the hospital and that's probably best too.'

'Lucy wants to stay,' Julia said from the door.

'We'll take Lucy then. Alex may not want to see anyone but you, Nell, in any case.'

Julia rushed out with her bicycle, but Rod had not waited. De-

58

pressed, she began to ride slowly to school. She dreaded facing people, people who would ask her what was the matter. Yet she had no desire to turn back home, nor did she want to be alone for long. She rode slower and slower, until she got off and walked along the pavement. Despair gripped her as it never had before; she felt frightened at the emptiness all round her life. The bicycle rattled on the pavement and she stared at the wheels going round.

'Julia Parrish. You're very late.' The headmistress happened to pass through the hall as she finally entered the school.

'I'm sorry, I . . . There was a problem at home.'

'Did you bring a note by any chance?' The head knew that Mrs Parrish was a reliable parent, meticulous about notes.

'I'm sorry.' Julia stared at her shoes. After a pause she added : 'My sister Lucy won't be coming in at all. She'll bring a note for us both tomorrow.'

'Fair enough. Is everything all right, Julia?'

'Perfectly, thank you, Miss Datchett.'

Perfectly, perfectly. A perfectly rotten mess. She went to the lavatory and then washed her hands, gazing at herself in the flyblown mirror above the basin. Brown eyes, brown hair; long nose and full, well-shaped mouth. She could see no likeness to her father at all except that their eyes were the same colour.

'Nell darling, I think it would be better if you went in by yourself. Lucy and I will wait outside and if Alex wants to see us—well, you can come and get us.'

'Perhaps you're right.' Nell did not know whether Connie was being thoughtful or cowardly, and was too exhausted to care. She ran her hand through her hair; it was lank and greasy, and there were large damp stains of perspiration under the arms of her cotton dress. She never perspired much normally. She left Connie and Lucy sitting on chairs in the corridor outside the medical ward in which Alex lay. As she walked down the long row of beds, the buzz of visitors confused her and she could not find him. She could feel herself trembling. She retraced her steps and saw Alex, fast asleep.

Nell stood helpless beside his bed; she had tried to imagine all sorts of bedside scenes but sleep had not occurred to her. Alex had pushed his bedclothes down, and was wearing hospital pyjamas which were grey with age. She noticed that none of the buttons matched and stared at these as if mesmerized.

Then she looked at his face, pale and drawn; his hair was damp with heat even though he was near an open window. Outside, pigeons flew through the clear blue sky, cooing and fluttering when they landed on the window-sill.

Nell put down the bag of things she had brought but did not open it. She sat down quietly beside the bed, and as she looked at his face, at the lines of his hair, ear and chin, at his familiar hands, her heart began to thud with retrospective terror. Precious, precious Alex, so nearly lost. The fear she had not had time to feel yesterday she felt now; her whole body began to shake and she wanted to be sick. She looked wildly round, afraid of breaking down. On an impulse she drew the cubicle curtains and then, kneeling, laid her face down on the bed well away from Alex and shuddered with sobs.

A nurse put her head in within minutes of the curtains being drawn; she saw Nell prostrate, and retreated leaving the curtains more or less closed. At the back of her brain Nell was aware of a nurse's voice saying: 'It's all right, his wife is with him.' Slowly she pulled herself together. Alex did not stir, and she wondered what to do. She tidied her hair and put some more lipstick and powder on, and pushed back the curtains. The rattle of the rings must have pierced Alex's sleep, because without moving his body he slowly opened his eyes. Nell sat down so that she was on a level with him and whispered his name. His eyes remained stunned and blank for a few moments, and then he blinked and expression of some sort returned. Nell kissed him on the forehead, unable to speak.

'My throat aches,' Alex croaked. He straightened himself and pulled the bedclothes up.

'Have some water to drink.' She held the glass for him and he sipped gingerly.

'It's painful to swallow.' He pushed the glass away, frowning.

'I expect the ache is caused by whatever they used to pump you out.'

Alex gripped her hand suddenly, and shut his eyes again. They sat in silence; it was broken by the clangour of the bell announcing the end of the visiting period. Alex looked stricken.

'But you've only just come,' he whispered.

'No, I've been here for ages. You were fast asleep.'

'You should have woken me.' He sounded so upset she thought he was going to cry. 'Stay a bit longer. I need you, Nell.'

So she sat still as the rest of the visitors left. But Alex said no more; he lay, grey-faced, with his eyes shut. Nell then began to unpack the things she had brought and stowed them in his locker. 'Oh dear, I've forgotten to bring any books. I'll bring some this evening.' A nurse came and asked her to leave. Doctors were entering the ward at the far end.

'Alex, I've got to go now. I'll see you this evening.' She kissed him again; he did not open his eyes. 'Is there anything you particularly need?' He shook his head. Nell walked quickly away.

'I wouldn't wind it up too often, Lucy. The spring isn't very strong.'

The bird had been singing on and off for the past hour. Connie was trying to read, and feeling increasingly irritated by the trills.

'I thought you said the spring was new.'

'But the whole apparatus is very fragile. I wouldn't strain it.'

Lucy put the cage on top of the television. 'I don't know what to do. There's nothing on telly. I wish the others would come back.'

'Read a book.'

'I can't settle to anything. I feel all miserable and edgy. Perhaps I'll go and ring up Betty.'

'Lucy dear, you haven't told Betty about Alex have you?'

'I haven't had a chance.'

'Well, don't. Nell and I feel that the wisest thing of all is to keep silence.'

'I know, I know. I won't tell.' She wandered over to the window. 'Here are Rod and Julia back at last. They're very late.'

Rod went straight upstairs and Julia came into the sitting-room. 'Where's Mum?'

'She went for a rest when we got back from the hospital and she's still asleep. Don't disturb her.'

'How did the visit go?'

'She went in on her own. Quite well, it seems. Alex was very tired. I think your mother plans to go back this evening.'

Lucy wound up the bird again and set it singing. Connie went into the kitchen, wondering what she should do to be of use. She felt flat and tired, and wanted to go back home. She opened the fridge and gazed blankly into it.

Julia came into the kitchen and poured herself a glass of water.

'How was school, darling?'

'Manageable. Just.'

Connie picked up a plate with the remains of a joint on it. 'This seems to be a possibility for supper. What shall we do with it?'

'Make a curry. Mum often does.'

'That's one decision made.'

Julia watched her cut up the meat without really seeing her; she felt so unreal, so detached from the humdrum conversation, from the details of ordinary living and the familiar kitchen around her. Her grandmother seemed far away, strange and insubstantial. Julia tried to focus on Connie's hands as she worked. That meat; that's the meat she had cooked for the magical dinner on Saturday. She turned away, rather frightened to realize only forty-eight hours had gone by since then. So much had happened.

Julia took her glass into the garden and sat down under the mulberry tree. Still stuck in a branch was her slipper; she had quite forgotten she had thrown it into the tree. She would get a stick and dislodge it, later. Later. Holding her glass of cold water against her forehead, she tried to relax, but peace of mind would not come. The mulberry tree rattled in the hot breeze, and she wished the heatwave would end; she was sure it would be easier to bear the blackness of life if the world around was grey and wet. She got up and went inside the house. Habit took her to the piano, which she usually practised at this hour. She sat down and played some scales and exercises absent-mindedly while staring at the stacks of music piled on the piano top. Mozart, Beethoven, Schubert, Chopin, Haydn. Bach. Bach, perhaps some Bach. She did not really like Bach, but today his structured order was what she felt she needed. She sight-read a prelude and fugue adequately, but the effort was unrewarding. Depressed, she shut the piano and wandered up to Rod's room.

It was empty. Rod had obviously slipped out of the house un-observed. His desk was piled high with text books and papers; he had unpacked his bag but got no further. Where was the blighter anyway? She flung herself on Rod's bed; it hadn't been made properly for days and felt lumpy. She lay back, aware of the faintly sweaty, earthy smell of Rod's sheets. Aimlessly, she gazed round the room.

Rod came in and went to the window, gazing blankly into the garden. The evening sun silhouetted his head.

'Where have you been?'

'I went to the Lord Nelson for a beer.'

'Oh.' She looked at the piles of books and dog-eared files. 'When are your exams precisely?'

'In three weeks' time.'

'I didn't realize they were that close.'

'It's a nightmare.' He spoke slowly, tapping on the window with a biro. 'Buzz off, Ju. I ought to be working now.'

As she went downstairs she heard him turn his transistor on. He usually preferred to work in silence, and was scornful of those who needed background music.

'I'll come with you to the hospital, Mum,' said Julia suddenly, as Nell was searching for the car keys. 'I'll come.'

'You sound as if you're getting the courage together to go to the dentist.'

'Shut up, Lucy.'

'Do come, my love. I wish I knew where I'd put those keys.'

'Unless you'd rather I didn't.'

'It would be nice if you came.' Nell rootled through the catch-all bowl of flotsam on top of the fridge. 'I could have sworn the spare keys were here. Aha—I was right. Come on then, Julia.'

'Why didn't Granny want to come with you after all?'

'Granny can only take so much, and she's tired. She hates hospitals and illness and broken bodies. I think she's rather frightened of what she may see in the ward. On the other hand, she's dying to see Alex. She'll come tomorrow. And to be honest, I think Alex will cope with her better tomorrow.' Nell was talking energetically as if to bolster them both up. 'He was asleep when I got there this afternoon. He only woke up at the end.'

'What's the ward like?'

'I hardly noticed.'

They drove in silence. Julia picked nervously at a wart on her hand, and Nell began to wonder if she had been wise to bring her. But she knew that Julia was Alex's favourite at heart, and that the moment when he faced his children again should not be postponed.

When they arrived in the ward, Alex was sitting up reading a newspaper, wearing his own pyjamas and his dark glasses. He looked so much more himself that Nell involuntarily smiled and quickened her pace.

Julia flung herself clumsily forward to kiss him, and knocked his glasses sideways. Before he straightened them she noticed how red and swollen his eyes were, as if he had been crying. She sat on the end of his bed, glad of the buzz of visitors' voices round them. Alex's hands shook as he folded up his newspaper.

'How's your throat?' asked Nell.

'A little better. It's nice to see my Julia.'

Julia smiled, unable to speak. The sight of her father sitting in a hospital bed, with his thin shoulders, dark glasses and pale face, brought back the agony of fear she had felt the night before. He sensed her pain and took one of her hands in his. He turned to look at Nell and said something which neither of them were able to hear because of the din made by a large aeroplane passing overhead, but Julia thought it was 'sorry'.

The noise of the aeroplane died away and, the tension broken, Nell and Alex began to talk about hospital matters. Julia sat back and looked round the ward.

Most of the men in it appeared to be elderly, but three beds away she noticed a dark young man on his own, conspicuously without visitors. He had his earphones on, but his eyes were watching the activity of the ward around him. His glance kept returning to Julia; aware of it, she shifted her position slightly so that she faced away from him. But she could feel the young man's eyes on her; she noticed he had bandages showing out of the sleeves of his pyjamas.

Alex's talk stopped. He took off his dark glasses at last and rubbed his eyes. 'When will my new ones be ready?'

'I'm terribly sorry.' Nell was remorseful. 'But what with one thing and another I haven't been to the oculist yet. I'll do that first thing tomorrow.'

'Oh *Nell*. Never mind. But these give me such a headache.' He lay back with his eyes shut; Nell put his glasses into their case and fussed about, tidying his locker.

'Granny sends her love,' said Julia, to fill the silence. She saw her mother's hands go still, and froze too. She had said the wrong thing.

'Mother?' Alex opened his eyes, alarmed. 'You haven't told her, have you?'

'We didn't mean to, darling, but she happened to ring up while I was out and Julia found she couldn't avoid telling her. It's hard to keep things in when you're upset. Connie came up immediately.'

'That's bad news.' Alex was distressed. 'She needn't have known at all—it will hurt her too much. I wish you hadn't told her.'

'She's taken it very well.'

'You ought to know by now how much she covers up.' Alex put his glasses back on.

'She brought Lucy's birthday present up with her,' said Julia. 'It's the most beautiful birdcage with a mechanical singing bird in it. Granny said it was Victorian.'

Alex was not listening. 'I wish you hadn't told her,' he repeated fretfully.

Julia longed for the visiting period to end; she saw by the ward clock there were five more minutes to go. She was getting pins and needles in her legs, so she got off the bed. The dark young man was still watching her; he seemed to be smiling in her direction. Or perhaps he was just smiling at something he was listening to.

Julia suddenly realized that Nell was dabbing at her eyes with a tissue, trying not to cry. 'Please don't go on about Connie, Alex. We're all doing our best to keep going.' Her hands were moving jerkily. At that moment a nurse rang the bell for the visitors to leave. Nell blew her nose.

'I'm sorry,' said Alex at last.

'We'll manage.' Nell smiled brightly to cover the pain she felt. She stood up beside Julia.

'Don't forget my glasses.'

'I won't, I promise.'

'I'll remind her, Dad.' Julia kissed her father, longing to escape now from the ward. Nell clearly wanted to escape too, because she left the hospital almost at a run.

'Hurry up, Ju, for God's sake,' she snapped, holding the car door open. Tears began to pour down her cheeks.

'What on earth's the matter, Mum?'

Nell sat down heavily on the car seat and wept, leaning her arms on the steering wheel. Julia patted her shoulder, feeling useless.

'Take no notice,' said Nell through her sobs. 'Everything's been too much. Bloody man. And he doesn't seem to care a scrap for what I feel, or for what he's done to us all. He's only interested in himself.' She blew her nose. 'We all have to bear the brunt of what he's done—as usual. So I can't help feeling a little bitter.'

'Poor Mum. It's been dreadful for you.' Julia unscrewed and screwed up the knob of the gear-lever. It was nearly dark now, and other cars were revving up and leaving all round them. Soon they were almost the only car left.

'I wish I could drive.'

Nell pushed her hair back and wiped tears away. 'Sorry about that outburst. Life has been appalling. But I'll manage. I'll have to.' She started the car, and it jolted and stalled.

'Calm down first, Mum. There's no hurry.'

They sat in silence. An ambulance, siren wailing, roared to the casualty entrance. They saw people bustling about its doors, and the sight of other people's activity was soothing.

'I said to Rod today, that I wished this week could just unbe,' said Julia. 'You know, that it could pass without us having to live through it.'

Nell sighed in the shuddering way habitual after a bout of crying. 'I know just what you mean.'

'Perhaps we all ought to go to bed for a week and just stay there.'

'Would that we could.' There was a pause, then Nell fastened her safety belt, decisively started the car and drove off.

When she arrived the next evening accompanied again by Julia, Alex's first words were:

'Why hasn't Rod come yet?'

'He's working hard for his A-levels, darling.'

'Surely he could spare an hour to visit his father?'

'He's really going flat out, Dad. The results of these exams are very important for his future, after all.'

'I'm well aware of that, but I'm sure he could find time if he tried. There's someone here I'd like him to meet.' Alex looked towards a nearby bed, the dark young man's, but it was empty. Alex went on in lowered tones: 'He isn't there at the moment, but I'll tell you about him. He's a very nice and rather lonely young New Zealander called Charlie Brenan. I've had several good conversations with him.'

'I had noticed him,' said Julia.

'He doesn't have anyone to visit him, his family's in New Zealand. I expect he's taken himself off because not having visitors must be a little painful for him.'

Nell had been unpacking various things from a carrier bag and stowing them in Alex's locker. She said with desultory interest: 'What's he in hospital for? I'd noticed him too.'

'For the same reason as I am.' Alex had his dark glasses on, and his eyes were therefore invisible. His voice was expressionless. 'He told me so himself.'

Neither Nell nor Julia found anything to say. They both felt a sense of shock, and were profoundly thankful that the boy was out of the ward.

'Mind you,' went on Alex, 'one could have guessed—he has two bandaged wrists.'

'I noticed that too,' said Julia, 'but I didn't guess. He kept staring at me.' There was a slight pause.

'Well, Alex dear, what's been happening today?' asked Nell brightly. They chatted on, but the atmosphere was uneasy. Alex was obviously on the look-out for Charlie, and Julia and Nell were hoping he would not appear. But he did, five minutes before the bell was rung. He kept his eyes to the floor as he hurried past Alex's bed, but Alex called out: 'Charlie! Come and meet some of my family.'

When Charlie saw Julia he blushed, but came slowly up to the bed. His dressing-gown, clearly home-made from rather ugly blanket fabric, was tied tightly round with a belt that did not match; the sleeves were too short, and revealed the bandaged wrists. He shook hands with Nell and Julia in a jerky, formal manner.

'Pleased to meet you.' Both Nell and Julia were struck by the contrast of his light, boyish voice with his tall, well-developed body. Julia smiled as warmly as she could to hide her discomfiture. She could not bear to look at his wrists.

'I also have a son, Roderick, who's about your age. With luck he might condescend to visit me too, and then you can meet him. My youngest daughter is called Lucy.'

Charlie stood stiffly, his hands behind his back.

'My husband tells me you're a New Zealander.'

'That's right.'

'Have you been in England long?' Nell's voice was warily polite; she was making a great effort to keep the conversation going.

68

'Eight months.' Charlie Brenan swallowed. 'Seems longer.' He looked appealingly at Alex, and Julia was surprised by the sweetness of the smile her father gave him.

'Charlie came to England to finish his training as a cabinet-maker. But he's had bad luck, haven't you, Charlie?' Charlie nodded. Nell turned away to Alex's locker, and began rearranging it.

'Would you like us to bring you anything?' Julia asked Charlie, who blushed again.

'I'm all right, thanks.'

The bell rang, and with another pleading glance at Alex, Charlie backed away and returned to his own bed.

As Nell and Julia left the ward, the sister-in-charge stopped them and said: 'Mrs Parrish? If you're not in a hurry the hospital psychiatrist would very much like a word with you—she's in the office here at the moment.'

Nell blinked fast, clutching her handbag. 'Now?'

'She's very busy, so you're lucky to see her. She isn't often available.' The sister smiled and herded Nell towards the door of a small room off the corridor. Julia followed closely.

'Do come in. I'm Doctor Rogers,' said a youngish woman with an attractive lop-sided smile. 'How nice to catch you. Have the only chair—I'm sure,' she added to Julia, 'you don't mind the window-sill. Now.' Doctor Rogers had a folder of notes open on the desk which she looked at briefly. 'I see there are two more of you—an eighteen-year-old son and a fifteen-year-old daughter.' She grinned at Nell. 'You married young.'

Nell smiled back in liking. 'Yes, I did.' They chatted for a minute or two before the doctor said:

'Have you ever during your long married life together been afraid that your husband might do what he did?'

'Yes, in the last few years the idea did occur to me.'

'For any reason?'

'About eight years ago my husband started getting bouts of severe depression.'

'Tell me about them.'

'They came on fairly suddenly and lasted several weeks. Then just as suddenly they would end, for no apparent reason.'

'What did you do to help him?' Doctor Rogers had a direct, friendly manner that kept Nell at her ease. Julia sat listening intently.

'What do a wife and family do, except keep normal life going as best they can? During these periods he isolated himself from us, and we tried to bridge this by being cheerful and ordinary.' She hesitated. 'I begged him to see a special doctor, without success.'

'What sort of doctor, Mrs Parrish?'

'He would only go to our GP, and that very unwillingly. I wanted him to see a psychiatrist. But Alex always says we can cure our own mental ills.'

'I see.' Doctor Rogers closed the folder, having made a quick note.

'I hope you didn't have any trouble talking to him yourself—' began Nell.

'Not at all. He couldn't have been more co-operative.' Doctor Rogers leant back casually in her chair. 'If you feel you can talk about it, Mrs Parrish, I would be most grateful to know why you think he was brought to the point of suicide. I'm sure dozens of reasons have been going round in your brain.'

Nell started to click the catch of her handbag on and off. Click, click. 'I wish I knew for certain.'

'Just guess. Whatever you think is valuable.'

'He's always been very bad at coping with stress and tension. He's just finished organizing a big exhibition which exhausted him.' Doctor Rogers nodded. 'But I don't think that's an important reason. I don't know, Doctor. I'm no good at getting him to relax. I wish I was. I only make things worse.'

'He wants to go back to teaching,' said Julia suddenly. 'That's what he really loves doing. The night before this happened, he talked about it.'

'But teaching helped to cause his depressions,' cried Nell. Click, click went the catch. 'By the end of a term he was so drained he had nothing left to give.' There was a pause, while Doctor Rogers

70

waited with her serene, encouraging expression. 'I know you will say his depressions are an illness, and nothing to do with his work.'

'I wouldn't presume to make any such judgment with my scanty knowledge of your husband's case.' Doctor Rogers smiled. 'But do go on—perhaps you could tell me a little about the pattern of events that weekend?'

Nell did so, and the doctor prompted her with gentle questions about their family life and habits. The ward sister interrupted them, and Doctor Rogers said regretfully : 'I'm very sorry, but I have to go.'

Nell looked upset. 'Oh dear. There's such a lot I wanted to ask you. Why—why do *you* think he did it?'

'Mrs Parrish, I'm in no position to judge.' She stood up. 'There are so many factors involved.'

'But would you tell us anyway?' asked Julia, and Doctor Rogers looked straight at her.

'Since you ask me, no, I wouldn't. I think it is important for you all to find out for yourselves.' She picked up a pile of folders and put them in a filing tray. 'But I would very much like Mr Parrish to attend my weekly clinic here after he is discharged.'

'You'll never get him to come,' stated Nell.

'You may be wrong, Mrs Parrish. He agreed to give it a try.' Doctor Rogers hesitated. 'He'll need all your support, which I know I can rely on since you realized his need for some kind of psychiatric treatment.'

'Of course.' Nell stood up. 'I won't tell him about our conversation—'

'Oh, please do. You see, he knows I was going to talk to you. I had to ask his permission, and he said it was an excellent idea. His very words.'

The ward sister tapped on the door and stuck her head in. Doctor Rogers waved her away again. 'I think Mr Parrish won't need long in hospital—a couple more days at the most—he could come out on Friday. The best thing possible would be if he could spend a few days outside London before he returns home; he's nervous of plunging straight back into the daily routine. It's a common reaction. I hope it can be arranged—Mr Parrish seemed to think there'd be no problem.' Doctor Rogers said goodbye and left. Nell and Julia made their way out; as they stood in a lift, Nell burst out:

'Where on earth can Alex go? I can't think of anywhere that would do in the circumstances.'

'What about Granny's?'

'He may not want to go there. You know how he always says Connie eats him alive when they're on their own together. But it's the obvious place. Damn it, he'll have to go there. And it'll be just what Connie wants, to have her little boy back home away from that nasty family of his that drove him to suicide.'

'Mum—'

'I'm being unfair, don't listen to me.'

Julia had to run to keep up with her mother. When they were in the car, she asked: 'What did you think of Charlie Brenan, Mum?'

'I must say it was the final straw, Alex bringing him over during our precious visiting hour. I don't mean that unkindly—the boy seemed very pleasant.' She sighed. 'It's just that I hadn't the energy left over to make conversation with strangers.'

'He had nice eyes.' Julia thought about their blankly vulnerable expression, and wondered what agony of spirit had made Charlie Brenan cut his wrists. After a pause, Nell cried:

'That doctor told us nothing. Nothing! Alex had obviously told her a lot. Why didn't she pass some of it on? It would have helped me to know what he'd told her.'

'Ask him yourself some time, Mum.'

Nell did not answer. They drove home in silence.

Connie went straight to St Jude's the next day to invite her son to stay. When she returned she was tense; Alex had made a suggestion which worried her and she was longing to talk to Nell about it. She opened the front door with the stiff spare key, expecting to find Nell alone. But Rod was with her; he had come home from school unexpectedly, giving no explanation. He and Nell were drinking coffee in the kitchen.

'Have some, Connie. It's freshly made.'

'I will indeed. I had a perfectly disgusting cup of tea at the hospital. I need to take the taste away.' Connie stirred her mug.

'How was he?'

'Cheerful. Full of plans.'

'Plans?'

'He wants to come straight down to Compton with me when he leaves the hospital. He also wants that young man in the same ward, Charlie Brenan, the one you met, to come too. Charlie is apparently very much on his own, and in a depressing bedsitter somewhere.'

'Who the hell is Charlie Brenan?' asked Rod.

Nell explained Charlie briefly; when she told him that Charlie was in St Jude's for the same reason as Alex, Rod turned away.

'It sounds crazy.'

'Julia met him yesterday. She quite liked him.'

'But the idea sounds *crazy*. How on earth is Granny going to cope with a suicidal young man she doesn't know, as well as Alex?'

Connie, who thought Rod sounded jealous, drank her coffee calmly. 'It might even make it easier. He and Alex seemed to have struck up quite a friendship. There's a sympathetic fellow-feeling between them; they both have, after all, experienced something which we can't share with them. No, Rod darling, mad though it sounds, I think there's a lot to be said for Alex's plan.'

'Surely this Charlie fellow has a family?'

'In New Zealand. He's on his own here.'

'I see.' Rod went and stood in the doorway into the garden. He did not like this latest development, but did not know why. But there was no aspect of life he liked at the moment. A spongy black cloud enveloped him and stifled all activity of the mind or spirit. The effort of thinking or concentrating was quite beyond him. He had walked out of school while ostensibly on his way to the science laboratory. He knew that he could not have summoned any of the patient, delicate attention needed to work on an experiment. So he had walked out, knowing he would be in trouble for it. 'I'm going to lie down in the garden. I'm not feeling too good.'

'You do that, darling. You look very pale.' Connie watched her grandson for a moment, and then turned back to Nell. 'I didn't like the idea much when Alex brought it up, but I've got used to it already. Don't look so worried, Nell. I'll get extra help from the village. Mrs Weekes would always lend a hand.'

'I don't know what I feel about it. I'm surprised that Alex suggested it, knowing him. He doesn't usually take people under his wing. I'd have thought he needs to go away on his own.'

'He was quite insistent. We talked while Charlie was out of the ward, and we also talked to him about it. Alex had already asked him.'

Nell paced about. 'Like Rod, I feel nervous about Charlie Brenan. We know nothing about him; you might be saddling yourself with an enormous problem. Say he—say he turns out to be very unbalanced and tries to do it again down at Compton.'

'I know, Nell, I know. But what can I do? Alex knows I have plenty of room for him. Both he and Alex seem very happy about the idea. They said the hospital was in favour, too. I can't say no, now can I? Imagine Charlie going back to a sordid empty room; that in itself might make him try again immediately. No. It would always be on my conscience.'

Nell cleared away the coffee things before she answered. 'I suppose Alex might feel the same.'

'Just so,' said Connie. 'That's what gave me courage.'

Nell could see she had made a supreme effort to adjust to this new development, and admired her for it.

Rod lay on the lawn, his headache pounding. He could hear the rattle of conversation in the kitchen, but not what was being said. He rubbed his forehead on the grass, misery filling him. He hated having his emotions rule him in quite this way; it had not happened to him before.

'What's the matter, Rod dear?'

His mother's voice beside him made him jump.

'I've got a ghastly headache.'

'Have an aspirin. I'll get you one.'

74

'It would probably be a good idea.'

Nell took two steps, and then laughed. Rod sat up, his headache bulging in his brain with the movement. 'What is it?'

'There isn't a single aspirin left in the house. It has its funny side.'

'Don't worry. I'll do without.' Then Rod too laughed, a dry, bitter chuckle that took hold of him and built up. He shook with it, his head on his knees. Nell went inside, disliking the noise he made. He had stopped when she returned with a glass and two aspirins.

'Connie had some. Come on, take them.'

'Thanks.' He put the two pills straight into his mouth, and drank off the glass of water. He then lay back, waiting for his mother to go. She hovered.

'Alex seems to have a good reason for asking Charlie Brenan to stay at Compton.'

'Mum.' Rod's words came out like his chuckle, soft and bitter. 'I could not give a damn what Dad thinks at the moment. I hate him for the pain and confusion he has caused; he never thinks of the effect of his actions on other people. If he wants to worry about this Charlie fellow first and his family last, let him; he's cut himself off from us all anyway by trying to escape us permanently. He's mucked us about so much I really couldn't care less if he stays down at Compton for months. We'd at least have a little peace.'

'Rod. Rod. Don't feel like that—'

'Please leave me alone, Mum. I don't want to talk about it any more.'

After a pause Nell said: 'Have a sleep if you can,' and went away.

Rod rolled over onto his front. Have a sleep. How could he; his thoughts were boiling in his head; as soon as he had circled through them once, he found he began again, and again. He lay rigid and unhappy. But the heat and the rustling leaves above him soothed him, the aspirin took its effect, and despite his lack of mental peace, he fell asleep.

5

When Carmen rang up the next evening, Julia was taken completely by surprise. The enormity of her family life had pushed even the Croxleys out of her mind.

'Carmen!'

'You sound as if you never expected to see me again.'

'Don't be silly. It's lovely to have you back. It's just that everything—that so much has been happening I'd forgotten you were due back.' She was aware of her mother standing beside her; Nell had appeared at Julia's happy cry of 'Carmen' and now had her finger to her lips. Julia covered the mouthpiece and said impatiently: 'I know, I know. I won't say a word. Don't flap.' Nell flicked her warningly on the cheek and went away.

'Did you get my postcard?' Carmen chattered on about the holiday and Julia half-listened, making appropriate noises. Other people's holidays were very hard to take in. Finally Carmen said: 'So what's been going on here, then?'

'Oh, nothing much.'

'But you said so much had been happening—'

'Not really, compared with what you've been doing on holiday.'

'Oh.'

Julia felt mean and awkward. She did not talk for much longer, because luckily Carmen had to get off the phone so that her father could use it.

''Bye, Carmen. It's great to have you back. See you tomorrow.'

Julia stood by the phone, fiddling with the springy plastic flex. She realized she had never had to keep a secret before. Those parts of her life which had in a sense been 'secret' she had told Carmen about because their friendship demanded it. Carmen discussed all aspects of her life in the frankest way possible, and Julia had found this novel and exciting, and responded. A secret was going to be difficult to keep, particularly if Carmen suspected its existence. Julia went up to her room, avoiding Nell. But Nell heard her, and called up the stairs : 'Do you know where Rod is ? I can't find him.'

'He went out.'

'But he said he was working all evening.'

'I heard him go out half an hour ago.'

'Oh, what is he up to ? He ought to be revising.'

Connie came up and took her arm. 'He's probably just gone out for some fresh air. It's a lovely evening. Come out for a turn round the garden.'

'I ought to pack Alex's things ready to go to Compton to-morrow.'

'There's plenty of time for that. Come on.'

'Thank God for Granny,' muttered Julia to Lucy. The phone rang again. 'You answer the damn thing this time.'

Lucy picked it up and heard the pips of a public telephone; whoever was ringing was evidently having trouble with the coins. Suddenly her father's voice burst through with a clatter : 'Hullo ? Hullo ? Who's that ?'

'Lucy. Hullo, Dad.'

'Lucy, hurry and get Nell, will you. This damn thing's playing me up, and I haven't got much change.'

'Hullo, darling. Yes, of course—quick, pass the pad.' Nell wrote down the long list of things that Alex wanted packed for the country.

'There's so much wouldn't it be better if you came here on the way from the hospital ?'

'No, no, you do it, please. It would be better to go straight from here.' The pips went and he was cut off.

'What was all that about ?' Connie stood beside her.

'Alex appears to want all his possessions packed.' Nell looked round-shouldered and dispirited. 'Perhaps you would get a couple of cases from the loft for me, Ju. One is not going to be enough.'

The telephone rang again. They all stared at it. This time Connie answered; they could all hear the pips, and then Alex's voice.

77

'Time ran out before I finished. Nell—oh, it's you now Connie —well, there's the question of Charlie's belongings. He needs some clothes, and he also says he left an envelope containing rent he owed lying about somewhere in his room. He's worried about it. This is the address; perhaps one of you could go along and see to things.'

Connie dutifully wrote down an address. 'Alex dear, this is all very well, but how are we to get into his room or flat or whatever?'

'The landlady in the basement has a key. She's a friend of Charlie's; she'll help, he says.'

'Very well, Alex. Yes. That's fine. Leave it to us.' Alex's call came to an end and Connie slowly replaced the receiver.

'We've got to get *Charlie's* things?' Julia was horrified; she had a mental vision of a blood-stained bedsitter. 'It's a bit much.'

'I nearly suggested that we should drive there tomorrow and collect them, but it seemed too complicated,' said Connie. 'We'll just have to do what they ask. It's the lesser of two evils.'

'It means going this evening.' Nell's face was drawn. There was a long pause.

'I'll go,' said Connie at last. 'If someone comes with me to read the map in case I get lost.' She looked at the girls.

'I haven't done my homework,' said Lucy.

Julia's heart sank. She hated Lucy, her father, the world in general; she was afraid of going to Charlie's room. 'I'll come,' she said, because there was no alternative.

'Then let's go at once.' When they were in the car, Connie went on : 'I believe in getting unpleasant things over and done with as soon as possible.' The trip was obviously costing her a great effort; her cheerful air was very forced.

It took them some time to find the address, because the house was on a corner with a side entrance. The dark steps to the basement were unlit and they fumbled their way down. A man came to the door immediately, and when Connie explained her errand he shouted over his shoulder: 'Joan! Some people come about Charlie.' He then left them waiting. A thin woman appeared after a few minutes and looked at them suspiciously. Connie explained again who she was.

'Why isn't he coming back here? I knew he was all right, I've been to see him at the hospital.' The woman was defensive.

'He is coming back after a week or so. He's just going to have a week's holiday. He asked us to get his things.'

'Did you say you was called Mrs Parrish? He never mentioned he knew anyone of that name.' The woman did not move.

'Charlie knows my son, he's in the same ward; the doctor asked if I could help out. I live in the country; Charlie would come with my son, who is also convalescing.' The woman, reassured, reached for a bunch of keys, and shouted at her husband that she was going upstairs.

'I found him, you know,' she said as she led the way. 'It was one of those lucky things. He'd borrowed a record off of me, and I wanted it back. Knew he was in, but couldn't get no reply. That wasn't like Charlie to keep quiet, usually he opened the door as quick as a flash, so I fetched the spare key and there he was, lying in a pool of blood. Never been so scared in me life. But the ambulance came quick and all I can say is thank God something sent me upstairs for that record. Otherwise he would have died. Definitely.'

'It was indeed lucky,' said Connie. By this time they were on the second floor; the house was a warren of bed-sitting-rooms, and smelt of combined cooking. Charlie Brenan's door had his name pinned up, but in large mirror-writing. The paintwork everywhere was battered. The woman opened the door.

Charlie's room, tight shut in the hot weather, smelt dreadful. By the little cooker in the corner was a half-full bottle of milk which had clearly gone off; there were some odd bits of food on a shelf which had also gone bad. Julia nearly retched; Connie had her lips pursed in a fixed smile and was breathing hard.

'Oh, my God,' said the woman. 'I did clean up the blood,' she added defensively. 'Just that bit there I couldn't get off. But they're supposed to clean their own rooms.' By the bed was a mark on the carpet which had been ineffectually scrubbed at. The carpet itself was stained and old, and ingrained with dirt. The bed, on which Charlie had obviously been found, had been stripped.

'Took his bedding to the launderette.'

'That was kind of you.' Connie smiled at the woman, who almost smiled back.

'It was the least I could do.'

They looked round the room, and found a suitcase on top of a cupboard. Connie looked at her list, and they began to put clothing, a pair of canvas shoes, and a few books into the case. All Charlie's clothes seemed to be hung on the back of the door; the cupboard was almost empty, and the unsteady chest of drawers was only half-full. Besides the few clothes and books, Charlie seemed to possess nothing. The walls were bare. The meanness of the room depressed Julia; she had never been into a cheap bedsitter before; what her friends called their 'bedsits' were in their own houses and a painful contrast to this room.

Connie checked her list. 'There's an envelope containing rent, apparently.'

'Haven't seen that.' The woman shook her head.

'And he particularly wants some little Maori charm, a green jade figure, small, on a chain. I've made a note here that it's "in a box". But what box?'

'Under the bed,' said the woman. 'I saw it there but I never touched it. As he turned out to be all right, there was no need.'

Far under the bed was a cardboard box; they pulled the bed out to get at it. The box was tied with a piece of string. Inside were two diaries, a bundle of letters mostly from New Zealand, an old silver-backed hair brush, a small box containing the imp-like jade charm, and two envelopes. One was marked 'Rent', and the other was addressed to his parents in New Zealand. The address was not complete. Connie gingerly picked up the first envelope.

'Do I give this to you, Mrs—?'

'Mrs Grayson. Yes, I'll take it.' She felt the envelope. 'His rent book's inside. Good.'

'Has he lived here long?' Connie did up the catches on the cheap fibre case.

'Six months, eight months. Something like that.'

Julia was looking at the crudely carved jade charm. 'It's a strange object.'

'Charlie said it was traditional Maori.' Mrs Grayson picked up the other letter. 'What shall we do with this? Typical Charlie to put a farewell letter inside a box under his bed.'

'Perhaps it's just a letter to his people that was already written before—' Connie stopped. 'I'll take it anyway and give it to him. He can then destroy it if necessary.' She looked at the rotting food and milk, and put her bag down on the bed. 'Come on, Julia, let's just clear away the mess, shall we? Perhaps we could have some old newspaper to wrap it up in? Where can we empty this bad milk?' She smiled at Mrs Grayson, who took the bottle from her.

'No, no. Please. I'll clear it up. I didn't clear his food away before because I thought it would serve him right if he came back to a mess, giving us a fright like that.' At last Mrs Grayson smiled. 'It wasn't very kind, I'll admit. I like Charlie really. I just didn't want to get involved. And the owner of this house is a real bastard, so I have to tread carefully to keep my job, like—'

'I quite understand. Finding Charlie Brenan must have been a great shock—'

'You can say that again.'

'Here's my address, where he will be for the next week or so. Perhaps you could forward his mail there.'

'Charlie never gets no letters, except one now and again from his family. I got one downstairs for him now, from New Zealand. Came this morning, funnily enough. I'll give it to you.' She led them out and fetched the letter while they were putting the case in the car.

'Tell Charlie I'm looking forward to seeing him next week, or whenever he gets back. And I'll give his room a good clean out.'

'Goodbye, Mrs Grayson.' Connie shook hands with her. 'I hope to send Charlie back fit and well.'

The hall seemed full of suitcases on Friday morning. The family were all going to the hospital to see Connie off with her charges.

Rod humped the cases into the car. He had not returned to the house until one in the morning, and refused to explain why; he was tired and bad-tempered.

'I shall be glad when this bloody farce is over,' he growled at Julia.

'You are in a foul mood.'

Rod went back into the house without replying. Privately, Julia thought her mother was a fool to insist on them all going to see Alex off. There was bound to be trouble from Rod.

'Julia. Come here a minute. I can't find that green charm of Charlie Brenan's. Did you have it or did I?' Connie had emptied her handbag out onto the kitchen table.

'Oh, Lord. What was I wearing yesterday? Jeans. It might be in one of the pockets.'

Nell sighed. 'I took the whole steaming pile of clothes off your chair this morning for washing—you'll find them on the floor in the laundry room.'

Eventually the charm was retrieved. By this time they were late, and Rod's temper grew worse. 'I've got to be in school by eleven; I've got a tutorial in my special subject and I can't be late. For God's sake everyone, get a move on. It's nearly ten already.' He went and sat in the car, opened a book and read all the way to the hospital.

Alex and Charlie were waiting in the main entrance door for them, and came out when the two cars drew up on the forecourt. Everyone except Rod was cheerful; the sun shone, although clouds were now giving signs that the heatwave was breaking. While Alex was talking to Nell and Connie, Julia gave Charlie his two letters and the charm.

'Your luggage is in the boot.'

'Thanks.' Charlie held the letters stiffly in front of him, but hung the charm round his neck. The eyes on the little jade figure were round red rings, blank in the middle; this gave the figure an expression of insolent, almost evil, surprise. Charlie's own eyes were puzzled and uneasy; he was tall, as tall as Rod, and his jeans and shirt were a little crumpled after their sojourn in his locker. He had squares of clean sticking plaster on each wrist.

Alex put his arms round Lucy's and Rod's shoulders. 'Nice to see you both before going to Compton.' Lucy smiled, and Rod tried to. He moved away from Alex's arm, looking at his watch. Nell prayed he would keep calm until the goodbyes were over.

'What about my spectacles, Nell?'

'I'll bring them down to Compton myself as soon as they're ready. The oculist said he would give them priority but it still takes time.'

'It's maddening coping with sunglasses all the time. I get such a headache.'

'I'm terribly sorry, Alex, it's rather my fault there's a delay—' but Rod, who knew Nell had forgotten to put the glasses on order immediately, broke in roughly :

'It's not your fault at all.'

Before Rod could say any more, Connie opened her car doors announcing brightly : 'Well, come on everyone. We seem to be causing congestion. In you get, Charlie; your case is already in the boot.'

Charlie hovered nervously. He seemed intimidated by the idea of being driven off to an unknown destination by an effusive and elderly lady. He looked pleadingly at Julia.

'Goodbye, Charlie. Lucky you going to Compton,' she said. Alex almost pushed him into the car. As Alex shut the door Connie asked him : 'Would you like to drive, darling?' But Alex, who usually hated being driven by anybody and particularly by his mother, shook his head. His face grew tense, and he turned and kissed Nell and the girls. He touched Rod briefly on the shoulder.

'Well, old fellow, look after them for me.'

Rod looked straight at his father's dark glasses. 'What can I do? It's your job.'

'You know what I mean.'

'Yes, I do. But I don't think you know what I mean.'

Rod turned and began to walk away. 'Goodbye. I'll find my own way to school, thanks.' He held his briefcase in the air in an ironic gesture of farewell. Alex got into the car. 'I hope Rod's not being a nuisance,' he said to Nell.

'Well, it's not entirely surprising if he's not his normal self.' There was a pause, then Connie started the car. Nell leaned through the open window to kiss first Connie, then Alex. 'I'll send Rod down to Compton as well if I get desperate,' she said lightly; 'I'm sure you'd love to have him in his present mood.' Connie raised her eyes to heaven.

Alex looked at Julia and Lucy. 'Don't you go playing your mother up as well.'

'As if we would.' Julia tried to joke, but it sounded false. As Connie drove away, she said to Nell: 'It would be his fault if we did.'

'That attitude will get us nowhere.' Nell slammed the car door. They drove off, and in a few minutes passed Rod waiting at a bus-stop. He either did not see them, or ignored them deliberately. Nell hesitated, and then drove on.

As soon as Julia reached school, Carmen rushed at her. 'Ju! Where have you been? I thought you were ill or something. It's great to see you.'

'It's great to see you.' The sight of her friend had given her a lift of the heart. 'Carmen, you look terrific, damn you.'

'All that lovely sun.' They found a quiet corner to talk in, and Carmen rattled on, making Julia laugh. Then she asked Julia suddenly, taking her off her guard: 'You looked miserable when you came in. What's happened?'

'Nothing, nothing.'

'Strange sort of nothing, if it makes you look so chewed up.'

'Oh, Carmen.'

'There *is* something wrong, isn't there?'

If Carmen had been curious, Julia would have stopped there, but Carmen only sounded concerned and worried. She even put her arm round Julia. All restraint went.

'We've had the most terrible few days. Few days. It feels like a lifetime.' She began to cry silently; Carmen comforted her. In the sheer release of tension, Julia found herself saying: 'On Sunday my father tried to kill himself with an overdose.'

'*Julia!*' Carmen looked stunned; she held her friend unable to think of anything to say. Over Julia's shoulder she saw another friend approaching and frowned off-puttingly. The girl left them alone. 'How dreadful for you all. Is he all right?'

'Yes, fine. He came out of hospital this morning. That's why I was late. Carmen, you must promise not to mention any of this to anyone, absolutely promise. I've broken my promise to Mum by telling you. You musn't let on to my family that you know. They'll be furious. I shouldn't have told you.' She blew her nose and pushed her hair back.

'Don't worry. I promise I won't tell a soul. I'm good at keeping secrets when I want to.'

'I thought I was.'

'Never mind, it's good that you've told me because now you can talk to me about it when you're feeling depressed.' Julia smiled at her, but was filled with misgiving. 'Oh dear, I shouldn't have told you. I did promise Mum.'

'But we don't have any secrets from each other anyway. That's a part of our friendship.'

Julia stood up, suddenly unsure whether this was what she really wanted from a friendship. She moved away, saying: 'I must go and get myself organized.' She opened her locker, and looked, unseeing, at the stacks of battered school books and files. She had broken her promise so easily. How could she have been so weak; the others would never forgive her.

6

'This really is the last straw.' Nell gazed in despair at the fallen plaster; Lucy had left her bath running full on all through breakfast (by chance a lengthier one than usual), and the water had poured through the cracks between the sanded wooden floorboards, saturating the sitting-room ceiling and bringing down a loose section of the moulded cornice. The water had run down one wall, seeping into a picture and soaking the area of carpet in that corner. For half an hour's overflow the damage was amazing.

'I'm sorry, Mum.' Lucy's face was bright red.

'How *could* you forget you'd started the bath? You never have one in the morning anyway. The weekend was depressing enough, but to start Monday like this—' Nell ran her hand through her lank-looking hair.

'I'm sorry. I suddenly wanted one, then I went to fetch my French verbs to learn in the bath, and then I got side-tracked. Oh Mum, I am sorry.' She was on the point of tears.

'Your birdcage escaped by a miracle.'

Plaster had fallen very near it, as it stood on a side table.

'Oh, this really is too much.' Nell flopped into a chair. 'I'll have to get a builder to look at the damage.'

'Leave the mess until this evening, Mum.' Rod was firm. 'Just *leave* it. We've all got to go now; we can't go on being late for school, but we'll all help you clear it up this evening.'

'That's right,' said Julia. 'Anyway, isn't Josie coming today?'

'No, she isn't.' Nell stared flatly at her children as they collected their bags of books and gear, a guitar and a tennis racket. 'Yes, you must leave or you'll be late. Off you go. I'll manage.'

'Please leave the mess.' Rod and Julia echoed each other. 'Please. We'll all help you this evening.' Nell seemed not to hear.

'Mum. Promise. Leave it.'

'All right.'

'Do something nice. Go out and see friends or an exhibition or something,' said Julia. 'Spend some money on a super dress.'

Nell got up and kissed her. 'Yes. Perhaps I will.' She watched the three of them leave, standing at the front door. She stood there after they were out of sight, staring blindly into the road. Then she shut the door and stood in the house, silent except for the odd, faint, dripping noise.

Lucy came home from school early, as was customary on Mondays. She let herself in with her own key; Nell was often out at that hour but usually came back soon after. She saw that the mess had not been touched, and though Nell had been told not to do anything, it was unlike her to leave it.

'Mum!' she called, breaking the silence, to establish the fact that her mother was out. Then she went through to the kitchen to make herself a drink of squash. There was broken china all over the kitchen floor: she stopped, shocked. Her first thought was of burglars, and then she realized that the mess consisted of their breakfast dishes only. It was all so inexplicable that she began to shake. She went out through the garden door and sat on the patio wall.

Now be calm, Lucy, be calm. (Ever since she was small, she had developed a detached and severe manner of talking to herself.) Just be calm and use your brain. Who threw all that china on the floor? No sign of a burglar. It must have been Mum. Mum. But why would she do such a thing? Oh dear, I wish—calm Lucy, calm, you must be calm. Perhaps she did it because she was so upset with all that mess—it was just too much to bear. That's it, that makes sense. She threw everything on the floor in a rage. But Mum doesn't usually do mad things like that. And why did she leave it all day, and where is she? Where?

Lucy's stern inner voice failed to keep her calm any longer. She wept for a while, until the cat jumped on her lap. Comforted by loud purring, Lucy slowly calmed down again. I must clear up.

That's what I must do. It'll be nice for Mum when she comes back to have it all tidy. I'll pick up the broken china, then I'll clear away the plaster. After all, the whole thing's my fault.

She hurried into the kitchen, and with an efficiency her family rarely saw, she cleared up the mess in the kitchen. Then she picked some flowers and put them in a bowl on the kitchen table. The cat would not leave her alone, and she realized it had not been fed yet that day, and promptly fed it. She then stood aimlessly, hoping her mother would now return, see the beautiful kitchen and be pleased and cheered; then they would clear the fallen plaster together. But Nell did not come.

Lucy then decided she would give housework a rest, and do some homework instead. She set out her books, but found she could not concentrate at all. Gloomily she gave in, and went into the sitting-room with a bucket and began to pick up the plaster. It nearly filled the bucket. She dusted the room, thinking as she did so: when I've done this I'll stop, if she's not back. But her mother did not come, and somehow she could not stop, so she even hoovered the sitting-room as part of her mental pact with her missing mother. She felt quite aggrieved when the whole job was done, and still she was alone. It was now four o'clock.

The telephone rang. She leapt at it, but it was only the oculist saying that Alex's glasses were ready. She looked vaguely for a pencil to make a note of this, could not find one, and forgot the message. She paced tensely up and down; each minute seemed to last for ever. The front door opened at last, but it was Julia. Lucy gazed blankly at her. Julia brushed by, going towards the kitchen.

'I see Mum's cleared up. I knew she wouldn't leave it for us.' Julia spoke with annoyance.

'*I* cleared it up. All by myself.'

'Well, you made the mess. I'm glad she made you do something for once.'

'She *didn't*. I don't know where Mum is. I cleared up of my own accord.'

'Wonders will never cease.' Julia smiled to herself as she put instant coffee in a mug, and swung the kettle onto the hotplate.

'I cleared up the mess in the kitchen too.'

'My dear Lucy, don't overdo things, you might strain yourself.'
Julia ate a spoonful of sugar.

'Shut up.' Lucy's voice broke. 'Don't be so horrid.'

'Aw, who's a poor little Cinderella. Come on Lucy, don't take
things to heart. What mess anyway; Mum always leaves the
kitchen tidy before going out. She couldn't *go* out if she didn't,
she's like that.'

'Well, she did. Oh Julia. All the breakfast things were smashed
on the floor.' Lucy burst into tears again.

'How? What do you mean? Had the table tipped over or something—for goodness sake stop crying and explain.' Amid sobs,
Lucy said: 'It looked asif Mum had smashed the lot deliberately
and then gone out just leaving it.'

'It needn't have been Mum.'

'Who else could it have been? The house was locked up. And she
didn't even remember to feed the cat.' There was a long silence.
Julia went outside, and Lucy followed. The kettle boiled un-
heeded.

'I decided she must have done it because she couldn't stand any
more after my awful bathwater disaster, and breaking the china
relieved her feelings.'

Julia did not answer.

'What do you think, Ju?'

'What? Oh yes, I expect you're right.' But Julia knew it was
worse than that. If you did something like smashing china to relieve
your feelings, you usually felt better immediately and then cleared
the mess up. Nell walking out on her disordered house was something quite different.

'What's today, Lucy? I've lost all sense of time.'

'Monday.'

'Monday. Rod has guitar today, and gets back late.' There was a
silence. 'Lucy, is the car there?'

'I never thought to look.' But she ran back to say it was not in the
garage.

'Perhaps Mum's gone down to Granny's. There might have been problems or something like that.'

'Oh *yes*. Of course that's where she'll be. Why didn't I think of that?' Lucy cheered up.

'It's only a suggestion.'

But Lucy had shuffled her worries off onto her sister, and was now examining her hands and arms. 'I'm covered in plaster dust. I think I'll have that bath I didn't have this morning.'

'Try and leave the rest of the ceiling intact this time.'

Lucy laughed, and went off humming to herself. Julia made her coffee, and then went to look in the dustbin to see how much smashed china there was; Lucy was a prime exaggerator. She saw that literally all the china which had been in use that morning was broken. She dropped the dustbin lid quickly. She did not understand, she did not understand.

The doorbell rang. This could be Nell—perhaps she had locked herself out. Julia flew to open it; there stood Carmen, whose smile faded when she saw Julia's face.

'What's the matter? More trouble?'

'I don't know what's happened to Mum.'

Carmen did not appear to hear. 'I was going to ask you back home for tea—' she hesitated.

'I'll have to wait here. Please stay, Carmen. Don't go off home.'

'Just for a bit then.' She followed Julia through into the garden. 'What's been going on?'

Julia told her. Carmen looked relieved.

'My mother often breaks things on purpose; once she smashed a plate so that Timothy and I wouldn't argue any more about who was to have it. She threw it on the floor in front of us. We were shattered.' Carmen laughed.

'But Mum smashed all the breakfast things while she was by herself. Come and look.' She showed Carmen the pile in the dustbin. Carmen did not seem very impressed.

'Well, that's probably got it all out of her system. A good therapeutic smashing.'

'Do you really think so?'

'Yes, I do. You're getting morbid because of what happened to your father.'

'I expect you're right.'

'I'm sure I am. As soon as she gets in ask her if you can come round to our place. OK?'

Carmen's unworried acceptance of the whole affair cheered Julia; she saw her friend off feeling full of affection towards her. It was only when Carmen had gone, and the house was silent again, except for splashing sounds from Lucy, that her cheerful feeling evaporated and she knew that in her heart she was still deeply worried. She wandered about, unable to settle to anything. The hands of the clock crept towards five; she found herself literally watching them. She made herself go outside and lie down under the tree, pressing her forehead into the lawn. Time passed.

'Ju.'

Her mother's voice seemed to come from inside her head.

'Ju? Want some tea?'

There was Nell in the kitchen door, voice and face as usual, everything normal.

'Yes, please,' answered Julia at last. When she reached the kitchen she saw that Nell was smoking; things were not as normal as all that. She could not remember the last time she had noticed Nell smoking.

'I'm glad we're on our own, darling.'

'Lucy's upstairs in the bath.'

'I know. She told me how she cleared up, the sweet thing.' Nell did not meet Julia's eyes. 'Let's sit down. I want to talk to you.'

Julia leant against the sink, so Nell remained standing. She put her cigarette down on a saucer; she was not enjoying it anyway.

'This morning something extraordinary happened to me, Ju, and I smashed all our breakfast china.'

'I know.'

'That I could do such a thing made me realize I'm at the end of my tether—I suppose this is how a nervous breakdown starts.' Nell's eyes shone rather oddly; she picked up her cigarette and put it down again. 'I've been to see various people today, besides having a good long think on my own. And I've come to a decision which I hope is the right one.'

Julia stared fixedly at the wart on her hand, pressing it with a fingernail. She was aware of her mother hovering tensely, but did not look at her.

'I need to get away, so I'm going off on my own. For a few days. I know I'm deserting you, but it's the only way. I can't take any more. I've spoken to Connie and she knows where I'm going. I know I'm doing the right thing, I know I am. Please tell me you understand.'

Julia went on examining her wart. It was getting bigger, she decided. She must have something done about it.

'Julia. Answer me.'

'Oh. Yes. It sounds like a good idea. We'll manage perfectly on our own, don't you worry about us.' Her voice was cool.

'Of course you will. I know you will. Josie can come in every day.' Nell tried to put her arm round Julia, who moved away. 'Darling, if I crack up it'll only make things worse. That's why I couldn't face going down to see your father yesterday.'

There was a silence, then Julia said :

'But I don't think we can manage if Dad comes home before you do.'

'Of course I'll be back first. I wouldn't dream of anything else.' Nell threw her cigarette away and drank tea. After a pause Julia asked : 'When are you going?'

'Tomorrow.'

The telephone rang, making them both jump. Julia answered it, and heard Carmen's voice saying imperiously : 'Well, aren't you coming?'

'Mum's just got in. I don't think I can.'

'Oh, go on. Just for a bit. My holiday photographs have come, you must see them.'

'Listen Carmen, she's going away for a few days tomorrow, so I really don't think I can. There'll be too much to discuss and arrange.'

'Is everything all right?'

Aware of Nell directly behind her, Julia said, 'Yes. Fine. See you tomorrow,' and rang off quickly.

Carmen was in mid-sentence when she was cut off. She banged the phone down. 'Blast Julia.'

Amy was passing. 'What's gone wrong, love? Julia usually lives here; I've never known her refuse to come.'

'She's in trouble.'

'I rather gathered that. Can we help her?' Amy was carrying an armful of dry sheets and towels upstairs, draped over her shoulders. 'I'm fond of Julia.'

'She's made me promise not to tell anyone.'

'There are occasions when that sort of promise is best broken. If she really is in trouble—' Carmen stared at her mother, in a genuine dilemma. Amy started up the stairs again.

'Don't tell me if you'd rather not. A promise is a promise, after all.' She went to the airing cupboard with the laundry. Carmen joined her a few minutes later.

'It's the whole family who's in trouble, not just Julia. She broke a promise when she told me, so perhaps she'll understand if I tell you.'

'Very likely.'

'While we were away her father tried to commit suicide. He took an overdose and was rushed to hospital.'

'Dear God.'

'And today when I went Julia was in a dreadful state about her mother. When they got back from school they found she'd smashed the breakfast china, and then just gone off leaving it. They didn't know where she was. I told Julia I thought she'd done it to get something out of her system, like the time when you smashed our plate.'

'Has she come back?'

'Apparently. Ju says she's decided to go off for a few days, so they'll be left on their own.'

'Where's their father?'

'Staying in the country with their grandmother.'

'His mother?'

'I don't know.'

'Poor Parrishes. Well, perhaps the children would like to come and stay here while their parents are away. Shall we ask them?'

'Oh, Mum, do let's. Not that Rod will want to, I'm sure. But— but we can't, because then they'll know I've told you all about it.' Carmen looked so upset that Amy put an arm round her.

'I'll tell you what. We'll wait until Mrs Parrish has gone, then I'll see Julia and explain that I insisted you told me what was going on, because I knew something was wrong and it worried me. Then we can offer help. How about that?'

'She'll still be annoyed.'

'But she can blame me, which will help.'

'Yes. I suppose so.' She followed Amy downstairs again to the chaotically untidy kitchen. There was a smell of bread rising. 'How dreadful to know your father tried to kill himself.'

'Not pleasant, I agree.' Amy took the cloth off the mixing bowl and began to knead the dough. 'But I think it's worth remembering that people sometimes try to kill themselves not because they're saying: "I hate you all, so I'm going to escape," but because they're crying out: "You should have *seen* how much I loved you, *understood* how unhappy I am."' She punched the dough vigorously, the bangles tinkling on her strong arms. 'Families are bad at taking each other seriously.' Carmen pinched off a piece of dough and ate it. There was a pause as Amy finished kneading, and plonked the dough into tins. As she washed her hands vigorously, Carmen said: 'Well, anyway, so you think it would be good to offer the Parrishes some help.'

'I do indeed.' She turned round, drying her hands on a tea-towel. 'We must. We must.'

7

Nell left very calmly. She had ordered a taxi for half past seven, and was ready to leave before her children were up or dressed. She woke them ten minutes before the taxi was due, and they stumbled downstairs yawning. The table was laid (with unaccustomed crockery) for breakfast, and Nell was smiling and efficient, but not quite herself.

When the taxi came, she kissed each of her children and left without flurry. They waved goodbye uneasily, and then shut the front door.

'She didn't mind leaving us at all,' said Lucy. Rod began climbing the stairs.

'Don't you want your breakfast?' Julia asked him sharply; she felt near tears.

'Later.' He yawned. 'Later.' His door shut.

'She didn't mind going at all,' said Lucy again, following Julia into the kitchen.

'Oh, don't go on about it. I'm thankful we didn't have any emotional scenes.'

Nell had left unusually little food in the house, so the girls began a shopping list for Josie.

'Let's get Josie to buy doughnuts for tea,' suggested Lucy. 'Mum never does. Rod adores them.'

'Me too.'

By the time Rod came down for breakfast the list was long. Rod glanced through it and laughed. 'While the cat's away.' He drank half a pint of milk straight from the bottle. 'Where's Mum put the kitty?'

'Usual place.'

Rod took down the cracked Toby jug. 'First place any thief would look of course.' He took out a roll of notes and removed three.

'What do you need that for?'

'I am going to lay in some booze for us deserted orphans. Guinness for me, and what about cider for you lot?'

Lucy's eyes gleamed. 'Mum's only been gone an hour and we've improved life already.'

Josie arrived, and stared at the devastated ceiling.

'Been bombed or something?'

'The bath overflowed with disastrous results,' said Julia, who had let her in. 'Dear Lucy forgot she had left it running.'

Josie came into the kitchen. 'Well, at least you're all up this morning.' She looked at Rod.

'Hi, Josie.'

'You look a bit brighter, not quite so hard on the eyes.' She went over to the Aga, where Nell usually left the breakfast pot of tea so that Josie could have a cup straight away before she started work. Josie frowned; she saw the three of them were watching her closely.

'Your mum ill or something?'

'She's gone off.' Julia knew it was unkind, but she enjoyed watching Josie control her expression.

'Gone off.' In Josie's world it meant only one thing. 'You're joking.'

'No, Josie, Mum's taken a holiday. She's gone off to get away from us all.'

Josie slammed the kettle on. 'Devils. For a moment you had me really worried, thinking that she'd gone off with a fancy-man.'

'Fancy-man.' They all repeated the word with delight and then began to laugh. They laughed and laughed in great cascades. Josie threw back her head and cackled, showing a mouthful of gold teeth.

'I say, Josie, look at all your gold teeth.'

'I know. Always said me mouth's me fortune.' She cackled again, and then coughed her racking smoker's cough. 'Gawd.

96

Laughing always sets me off. How's your dad? Has he gone off too then?'

'He's with Granny.' The laughter faded and the atmosphere slid into unease.

'Gone back to mother, eh.' Josie examined the three of them ironically. 'What's been going on?'

After a pause, during which Josie made a pot of tea, Julia said: 'Dad tried to commit suicide last Sunday. He's just come out of hospital and gone down to Granny's. We were trying to keep the whole thing secret.'

Josie stared at them in a long silence, busy with her thoughts. Then she poured herself some tea, picked up the shopping list, and said briskly: 'So this is what I've got to get for you, is it? Would you kids like me to move in while your mum's away?'

'Lovely, lovely Josie.' The three came back from school to find order, stores in, food prepared, and a note saying: 'See you in the morning.' All three of them were drenched by a sudden torrential electric storm; the rain was still beating down, and the light outside was a curious yellow.

Rod lifted the lid off a casserole. 'Gluey stew. Josie's no cook. It looks disgusting.' He dipped a finger into it. 'It tastes disgusting. Cook us something instead, Ju.'

'No. It won't kill us to eat that.' She looked into the pot and sniffed. 'Bisto and flour.'

'Take the meat out and start again. You're such a good cook. Josie'll never know.'

'I said no. I don't feel like it. I'm fed up with being a good cook.'

'Beast.' Rod took three bottles out of a carrier bag. 'These will improve the taste of Josie's stew.' He put the beer and cider on the table. 'Let's eat at about seven.' He went upstairs to work, but Julia heard him playing his guitar. His bag of books were left in the hall, and long before seven he was down again, watching a Western on television.

They took their supper into the sitting-room, a thing Nell never allowed. They had no sooner helped themselves to platefuls when the doorbell rang. Lucy peered out through the window.

'It's Carmen and her mother.'

'Oh, Lord.' Julia went to the door; rain was still beating down, and Amy and Carmen came in with a flurry of umbrellas.

'Julia, dear,' began Amy, 'forgive us for dropping in but we've come round to see if you need any help—'

'I had to tell her,' interrupted Carmen. 'I'm sorry, Ju.'

'I made her tell me—don't blame Carmen.' Amy saw Rod standing barefoot in the sitting-room door, a scowl on his face and his plate of food in his hand. 'Oh, I do apologize, you're all having supper. Please don't let us stop you.'

They made an awkward group in the sitting-room. The smell of Josie's stew filled the air.

'Who's the cook, Julia? You?' asked Amy.

'Our domestic help.'

'This stew's awful,' said Lucy. 'Josie's put in far too much salt.'

'Well, we came to ask you all for supper tomorrow night,' said Amy. 'It looks as if the offer's rather timely. Indeed, come every night while you're on your own.'

'That's very kind of you—' began Julia.

'It's the least I can do. And if there's anything else I can help with, you won't hesitate to ask, will you? I really mean that. You must all still be feeling very shocked.' Though Amy said this in a gentle, sympathetic voice, Julia prickled at the intrusion.

'We're managing all right, thank you.'

'I'm sure you are.' She glanced quickly at the saucepan and dishes on the carpet. 'But meals out are always a nice change—so we'll expect you tomorrow any time after six. Timothy's home, so you'll have some male companionship, Rod. I won't interrupt your meal any longer—come on, Carmen—'

'Couldn't Carmen stay for a while?'

'Oh—'

'Go on, Mum. I'll find my own way home.'

'Well, don't be late.' Amy smiled at everyone, took the umbrella, and left.

'Have some cider, Carmen,' said Rod, turning the television back on with his toe. He belched, and continued to eat his stew. Carmen sat down beside him and watched the film with exaggerated interest. Rod took little notice of her comments, but Julia could see he was enjoying her company. After an hour or so Julia went upstairs, hurt that Carmen was ignoring her, and bored by the programme they all seemed to find so amusing. She suddenly missed her mother with a piercing ache.

She went into her parents' bedroom, and stood for a moment looking round. Nell kept their bedroom tidy, serene and empty of evidence of her children. There was a green velvet chaise longue at the end of the bed; Julia lay down on it and shut her eyes. She could smell the faint individual scent of her mother as she turned her face to the soft velvet upholstery. Downstairs, the others laughed noisily. Julia started to cry.

As her tears dried she continued to lie on the chaise longue, thinking about her parents. Alex's shoes were tucked under the wardrobe; apart from these there was little evidence of him, except for a photograph of their wedding day.

Julia got up and stared hard at it. Her mother was wearing a very full dress, with a beautiful old lace veil. Her hair was pulled off her face, and though she was smiling she looked as if she was listening for something. Julia picked up the photograph in its silver frame. She knew that Nell had been nineteen when she got married, and it gave her a shock to realize that this cool woman was almost the same age as Rod. She looked more closely at Nell's face. Except for that listening attitude, it gave away no secrets, whereas Alex's face showed all—that he was nervous, vulnerable and very happy. His grin was slightly idiotic; Julia smiled involuntarily as she looked at him. He clearly loved Nell, but there was nothing in Nell's face to show she loved Alex. Julia covered the dress and veil with her fingers, and looked again at the face. You would never guess that face was on its wedding day, thought Julia. It looks like someone in a pleasant place enjoying the view, and listening out for a whistle or a call or a note of music. Alex looks like a person who has just got married; even a stranger seeing that grin might have guessed.

Next morning, Connie rang up. Julia answered, and stood swinging her school bag impatiently as her grandmother asked how things were going.

'Fine. How are you all getting on?'

'Not too well. I'm finding Charlie a bit of a problem, to be honest. He's at a complete loose end down here in the country. He's obviously bored stiff.'

'Oh dear.' Julia signalled to Lucy not to wait for her. 'That's annoying.'

'I feel that it's hindering Alex's recovery to have this bored restless young man around. They're out at the moment. Alex just wants to read and rest most of the day, and go for the odd walk. Both he and I are only too aware of Charlie hanging miserably around.'

'What can you do about it? Send him home?'

'I wish Nell hadn't gone off. You couldn't come down here for a day or two could you? You or Rod? Or even Lucy?'

Julia was filled with horror. 'What about school—we've all got exams, and Rod's are extremely important—'

'Of course, of course. Well, never mind, I just felt rather desperate, but I expect today will be better. It isn't that I dislike the boy; I like him. But I do want to be able to concentrate on my Alex.'

On the way to school—by now very late—Julia had what seemed to be a brilliant idea. Amy Croxley had offered to help; well, now there was something she could do. All day Julia chewed over her idea, but did not mention it to Carmen because she wanted to discuss it with Rod first.

He was dubious. 'Charlie might knife them in their beds.'

'Oh, Rod. He's more likely to knife himself.'

'I'm not surprised Granny can't cope. I said it was a mad idea to start with.'

'She said she wanted to concentrate on Alex—'

'Yes, I suppose it's not every day that your son attempts suicide.' His sarcastic tone upset Julia. She followed him upstairs, pressing him for a response to her suggestion that Charlie stayed with the Croxleys.

'Ask Mrs Croxley by all means if she'll have him. I'm not coming this evening, by the way, so please make my apologies.' Rod's eyes looked tired and empty.

'Why aren't you coming? You said you would.'

'Too much work.'

'There's nothing to eat here; we told Josie we'd be out tonight.'

'I'll get some fish and chips.' Rod shut the door of his room firmly. Julia sighed. She needed to talk to Rod; she needed his support. She could hear Lucy messing about in her room, but she did not want to talk things out with her; Lucy was too heedless. Julia went to her room and stared blindly into the garden. Life is full of decisions with important consequences, and I'm not able to make them. Perhaps I won't mention Charlie to Amy Croxley. Perhaps I ought to for Granny's sake. Oh Lord—

'Are we going?' Lucy stood in the doorway, twisting a necklace with her fingers.

'Yes. Rod isn't.'

Both Carmen and Amy were obviously disappointed that Rod had not come. Timothy came bouncing down the stairs; as usual, Julia felt herself grow tense and tongue-tied the moment she set eyes on him. It was stupid to feel so strongly in the face of a total lack of encouragement. Timothy said hullo in a friendly way, but looked with greater interest at Lucy, who was at her dreamy pre-Raphaelite best this evening. Julia left Carmen, Timothy and Lucy talking together, and followed Amy into the kitchen.

'Now, before I call the others, Julia, please tell me—is there nothing I can do to help you all? Life can't be easy for you at the moment.'

'Well, there is something I've been wondering whether I could ask you—'

'Ask away.'

'It's such a big thing I'm not sure it's fair to involve you—'

'I can always say no.' Yet Amy was a person who rarely said no, and they all knew it. Julia told her the story of Charlie.

'If Mum hadn't gone off I'm sure he would have come to stay with us—'

'Then why doesn't he come and stay here for a few days? That would solve the problem, wouldn't it?'

'That's what I was hoping, but it seemed crazy. You don't even know him. We hardly know him ourselves—' Julia tailed off.

'Don't worry, he can certainly come here. It's an excellent idea. And he's much the same age as Timothy, so perhaps that will help too. Not that Tim will be around for very long—he's just about off to America.'

'America?' Julia repeated blankly. 'I didn't know he was going to America. He won't want Charlie in the house for his last few days—'

'Oh, he's only going on some university theatrical tour. Tim, come here a minute. We need your advice.'

When Timothy heard about Charlie, he said: 'He sounds just the sort of person one can actually help. For once our philanthropic urges needn't remain theoretical.' He even offered to drive down and fetch Charlie from Compton, and it was finally arranged that he would take Julia with him.

Rod lay on his bed, the parcel of fish and chips open beside him. He was reading a pulp thriller; he had bought three that morning, because he knew that in his present state of mental inertia he could cope with nothing else. His work that week had been disastrous; he withered at the thought of how much he had not covered. He looked at his watch: only seven o'clock. For a moment he wished he had gone with the others. He ate a couple of chips but they were now cold and nasty. He crumpled up the packet and laid it on the floor. He picked up his thriller and began to read it, when the doorbell rang. He was tempted to ignore it, but it rang again. A totally strange middle-aged man smiled nervously at Rod when he opened the door.

'I'm Mr Thompson, the oculist. I happened to be passing your door, so I thought I would drop these in.' He held up a small parcel. 'Mrs Parrish said they were urgently needed, so I was a little puzzled no one came in to fetch them yesterday.' He spoke in a neat, unhurried voice, slightly apologetic in tone. 'I left a telephone message that they were ready.'

'It's very kind of you. I'm afraid my mother was suddenly called away yesterday so that was why she did not come in for the glasses.'

'Mr Parrish is not here, I take it? It would be useful to try them; sometimes the frames need adjusting.'

'No, he's away too. I'm sorry.'

Mr Thompson handed over the glasses with a gesture like a small bow. 'Well, I hope these are satisfactory. Tell him to contact me if they are not.' He smiled a singularly sweet smile, got into his old Morris Minor and drove off. Rod remembered Nell saying what a nice helpful man Mr Thompson was. He held the packet containing Alex's new glasses in his hands, and stood wondering how a man could be so happy and fulfilled being an oculist. His reverie was interrupted by the telephone ringing. He slammed the front door shut and swore. It was Julia.

'I get no damned peace. A man's just come to the front door to deliver Dad's glasses and now you ring up.'

'Sorry to disturb your lordship, but I need Granny's number. The Croxleys are going to have Charlie Brenan to stay—how about that?'

'Bully for them. They must be crazy.' He gave Julia the number, and rang off roughly. 'Now perhaps I'll get some peace and quiet.'

He did, but he found after an hour or so that peace and quiet was not what he wanted. The thriller failed to keep his attention, but a single sentence caught his eye:

' "That is the most selfish act I have ever heard of," cried Lucinda angrily.'

Rod threw the book aside. The most selfish act I know of, he said aloud, is my own father's. Suicide is the supremely selfish act—sod him. Sod him.

He rolled off the bed, grabbed some change, left the house and went quickly down the road to the pub. He bought a half of bitter, and went outside with it.

He leant against the brick wall of the pub and shut his eyes. How nice public places were; no special demands on you, no one eating you alive. With luck, university would be like that. He could not wait to get there.

8

Timothy Croxley's car was a very old MG; the hood was full of holes, and the engine noisy and unreliable.

'What a blissful car,' said Julia as she settled into the lumpy seat. 'And specially when I should be at school.'

'I must say I'm fond of it.' Timothy wore glasses to drive, plain black-rimmed ones, and they hardened the effect of his pale features. 'It's silly to feel affection for a car, but I admit I do.'

'Oh no, it's quite understandable. Particularly such a nice old car as this.'

Julia had woken up that morning with a feeling of dreadful, joyful anticipation. Her uppermost worry was simply the one of finding enough things to say on the journey down to Compton. But Timothy was friendly and unintimidating, and as soon as she asked him about his theatre trip to the United States, he talked for the next half hour. Then he asked her about Charlie. 'Come on, give. What's this guy like?'

'Large and muscly, but somehow like a small boy.' She thought hard. 'He looks as if he's the sort of person life will always hurt. I only met him twice, but you know how strong impressions can be. It's as if he hasn't grown a skin which most people have.'

'I know just what you mean. That's very perceptive. Some people do lack an emotional skin.'

Julia basked in Timothy's appreciation. He was wearing a blue and white striped T-shirt which looked very good on him; she could not help feeling pleased at being in a sports car with someone as attractive as he was.

'I hope Charlie's tough enough to stand up to Amy. She's liable to smother people if she thinks they need help.'

'He seemed a very lonely person, so I'd have thought her attention would please him.'

'Perhaps. You don't know my mother when she's in full philanthropic flood.'

They arrived at Compton without mishap, despite the fact the old car inexplicably stalled twice. Connie greeted them warmly, and led them through to the courtyard at the back. Her house had once been a stables, and the courtyard remained the heart of it, and the hub of Connie's life; she lived, ate and even on warm nights slept in it. Charlie was stretched out on a daybed half asleep, Alex was nowhere to be seen.

'He was here a minute ago.' Connie looked fussily around. Charlie swung to a sitting position, his hair on end.

'Hi, folks.' He beamed.

'How do you do.' Timothy shook hands, formally; Julia thought he looked put out by Charlie. There was even more of Charlie than she remembered. The plasters were off his wrists, and the scars looked very pink. Timothy obviously noticed them.

'Where's Alex, Charlie?'

'Gone off.' Charlie waved a hand in the direction of nearby woods. 'Couldn't stand the sight of me any longer.' He laughed.

'Well, let's all have a drink before lunch,' said Connie in what Julia would describe as her brave voice.

'May I help?' Timothy, narrow and fine-boned compared with Charlie, was at his most charming.

'How nice of you. Yes please.' She and Timothy went off together and Julia heard her telling him all about the house.

Julia went to the fence and called Alex. Her 'cooee' floated away, unanswered. She went back and sat down near Charlie.

'Alex is always going off walking. I only like to walk to get some place, but he just likes to walk.'

'I like it too.' Julia lay back in the sun. There was a long, awkward silence, until Alex appeared, coming out through the house.

'Dad!'

'Hullo, bunting.' He hugged her.

'We thought you'd gone off for a walk.'

'I did—just through the fields and back down the lane.' He took off his dark glasses and rubbed his eyes. This reminded Julia, and she triumphantly handed him his new glasses. Alex took them almost reverently.

'My goodness, are those welcome. Dear friends, let me put you on.' There was a pause as he readjusted them on his nose. 'Well, Julia, how are things at home?'

'All right. A bit shambolic, but we manage. Josie keeps us in order.'

'Of course, there's Josie.'

She could tell her father was not very interested in how they were coping. She noticed as she talked that Charlie was watching her, biting his lips nervously. It suddenly became clear to her that she had fixed up for him to go to the Croxleys without considering him or his wishes at all. She disliked herself for it, and smiled at him. But he had turned away, and did not see her smile.

'By the way,' said Alex, lowering his voice, 'Charlie and I have discussed his moving from here, and he agrees with me that it's too much for my mother at her age to have both of us convalescing. She's a highly-strung person and won't relax, so it makes things doubly difficult.'

Charlie looked round. 'I'm just a dead weight as far as she's concerned. I'm not used to this sort of life and she knows it.'

'My mother has always been a little inflexible—' Alex stopped, because Connie and Timothy were coming out of the house with a tray. Julia felt agonized on Charlie's behalf, and again tried to catch his eye; but this time he was staring down at his feet. It was only later, after lunch, that she had a moment to say to Charlie: 'You don't have to go from here to my friends the Croxleys if you don't want to.'

Charlie swallowed and gazed into the distance. 'I don't really care what I do next,' he said.

'They're very pleased about having you to stay.'

'Are they?' His eyes met hers briefly, empty of expression.

'I ought to be leaving soon,' said Timothy, coming up behind them. Alex followed, and put a hand on Julia's arm. 'Stay, Julia,' he said. 'Stay tonight and take an early train tomorrow. There's a commuter train which would get you to school more or less on time.' Julia gazed wordlessly at him.

'*Do* stay, darling.' Connie smiled encouragingly. Julia swallowed. She desperately wanted to travel back with Timothy; at last they were getting to know each other and she was looking forward to another couple of hours in his company.

'I don't want to let Timothy down—' she began lamely.

'Oh, don't worry about that. Actually, it would be better if you didn't come—there'd be a terrible squash in the MG with three of us and Charlie's luggage.' Timothy grinned.

'There you are, Ju. All settled. We'll swap you for Charlie.' Julia felt cold, depressed, let down by the casual way Timothy had dismissed her from his carload. He did not seem to mind at all. What had she expected, anyway. She watched as they loaded up the car, feeling sick at heart. Timothy turned and waved cheerfully from the gate, still shouting his thanks to Connie.

'What a nice young man Timothy Croxley is,' began Connie.

'Well, this is very pleasant.' Alex put his arm round Julia. 'Pity the other two aren't here as well. How is Rod?'

'Not quite his usual self.'

'Exam nerves, I expect.'

Julia moved away from Alex's arm; she wanted to shake him. She went quickly back into the house and up to the attic room she always slept in when staying with her grandmother. Charlie had been sleeping in it; the bed was rumpled and the window tight shut. Julia flung open the window and ripped the sheets off the bed. Charlie had left some magazines lying about, and Julia stuffed these into the wastepaper basket. She emptied the ashtray, noticing that Charlie's plasters were amongst the few stubs. When she had finally removed all trace of Charlie, she went downstairs again. Connie was asleep on the daybed in the courtyard and Alex was reading in the shade. Birds were picking up crumbs off the paving stones, and the only sound was a cow lowing in a nearby field.

Alex put his book down when he saw Julia. 'Could you bear the thought of a walk?'

'My shoes aren't very sensible.' They were her best sandals worn in honour of Timothy.

'Borrow a pair of Connie's. Her outdoor shoes are all in the hall.' With an extra pair of socks, some brogues fitted Julia not too badly. She and Alex set off through the wood up to a ridge of hill. Compton was on the edge of a large estate, and Connie had permission from the owner to walk in it. They went through a gate marked 'Private' into lush, overgrown, mixed woodland.

'I tried to bring Charlie here, but he wasn't keen on wading through undergrowth.' Alex's tone was dry.

'I don't think Charlie found the country to his taste.' They walked quietly, watching out for birds and wildlife. Alex went ahead; he was wearing a very old shirt dating from his college days, part of the collection of old clothes he kept down at Compton. Somehow the sight of him in his tattered shirt and aged trousers touched Julia, and she was very glad she had stayed on. When they reached a particular vantage point with a splendid view they stopped and sat on a large rounded rock which they had always called Elephant's Back. Alex and Julia gazed at the view in companionable silence.

'It's a long time since we've had a picnic here. Years,' said Julia.

'I wanted to bring one here with Connie and Charlie but neither was enthusiastic.'

'Granny usually loves these woods.'

'I think she didn't want to come here with Charlie.' Alex was tapping a stick against his leg as he spoke. Silence fell again.

'Why didn't Granny get on with Charlie?'

'I came to the conclusion that she was determined not to. And you know what a snob she is—she found his very different New Zealand background and his desire to become a cabinet-maker too much to assimilate in a "house-guest", to use her phrase.' He prodded his stick into the earth. 'I shouldn't have suggested it. I thought I needed a buffer between her and me. And Charlie himself is so much on his own and in need of help. It seemed sensible at the time.'

'Perhaps I interfered too much, arranging for him to go to the Croxleys.'

'I'll tell you something, Julia—I think he was so touched that you had bothered to do something for him he would have gone anywhere to please you.'

'He certainly didn't give me that impression.'

'He's very unsure of himself.' There was another silence. 'I'm hoping to help him find a job. Through the craftsmen's exhibition I got to know of several firms who might be interested in an apprentice. It's one of the first things I shall chase up when I get back to work.'

Julia killed a gnat against her arm. 'I can sympathize with Granny in a way.'

'What do you mean?'

'It's hard for us to understand what you see in Charlie.'

'It's hard enough to explain. It's not just because he needs help, or because he and I have shared an extreme experience.' Alex's eyes were shut. 'When he first came up to talk to me, I wanted him to go away. Almost the first thing he said was that we were both in hospital for the same reason. I felt as shocked as if he had thrown a bucket of cold water all over me. I hardly answered and he went away. Later on I saw him lying on his bed, staring at the ceiling, and I felt such a sense of compunction at my rudeness to this lonely boy, I went over and made friends. I discovered he is rather special —even though life has hurt him badly he is open, trusting, vulnerable; he doesn't envy or judge other people, or have any preconceptions at all. In a curious way, talking to Charlie is what I imagine talking to a saint would be like. Not that I mean he *is* a saint, of course . . .' Alex trailed off, frowning.

'What's Charlie's story?'

'His father is the manager of a sheep farm, with little time for family life. He has four older brothers; he should have been a girl and his mother obviously regretted she had no daughters. He left school early against his parents' wishes and became apprenticed to a cabinet-maker, an old man who became a father figure to him. Charlie obviously adored him, and was shattered when he died suddenly last year, at his work bench. Charlie said he had just made him a mug of tea. He left Charlie five hundred pounds, so Charlie decided to come "home" and finish his training with the firm who had trained the old man, somewhere in Kent.'

'What happened?'

'Charlie found that the firm was no longer in existence. His whole stay in England had been full of unhappy accidents, and he didn't have the strength of character to cope with them all on his own.'

'Poor Charlie. Doesn't he have any relatives in England?'

'An aunt in Lowestoft, who came to see him in hospital. They don't get on, and it doesn't surprise me. She looked a most joyless woman.'

Throughout this conversation, Julia could not control her slight resentment at her father's interest in Charlie and his life. She fidgeted unhappily.

'I have a bond with Charlie, which would remain even if I never saw him again. When I was at my lowest ebb he happened to be there, a perfect listener, and I could talk to him completely freely, as one never could to one's own family.' Alex looked at Julia. 'I explained to Doctor Rogers that of all my family, you were the person I could talk to, though; Nell hates it if I try to talk like this to her.'

Julia sat in a turmoil of emotion. She wanted to shake her father, but she understood him; he was arrogant and selfish, but she loved him. She stood up roughly.

'I'm getting bitten.' She flapped at a group of gnats. 'Let's go.' But Alex pulled her down again. 'No, don't let's go yet. It's so nice to talk.' Julia scratched her gnat bites and waited. 'Did you like Doctor Rogers?' he said at last.

'Yes.'

'So did I. She asked me to go to her therapy group; she suggested both Charlie and I attend it together for a while.'

'You will go, won't you? Dad?'

'I expect so.'

'You must.'

'I'll see. She's good, though; she's the first person I've ever met who has made me feel that not being able to cope with oneself is a fairly ordinary problem which needs helping. I had already seen I could not cope, but my solution was a trifle drastic.' Julia sat very still, listening to her father's wry voice. 'The paranoid, possessive, unstable father, given to bouts of serious depression, unable to find any true peace of mind, unfulfilled in his work, convinced that all happiness is merely illusion : there you have Alex Parrish, on what could have been the last Sunday of his life.'

'Don't, Dad, don't.'

'Shall I try and tell you why I did it?'

'I'm frightened of knowing.'

'So am I. So am I. I know all the obvious causes, including the heat, the hangover, and my broken spectacles. All so clear, but not the whole answer. I don't know the whole answer. I do know that an important part of it lay in my sense of isolation—I often feel isolated from everyone about me, but that particular day was exceptional. I was in a cold wasteland all alone, with only one way of escape.'

'But we had such a good evening together that Saturday.'

'Perfect. I know. The next day was all the more terrible by contrast. I began to feel as if the air around me was full of the beating wings of devils.'

Julia picked desperately at lichen on the grey rock. 'Please don't go on, I can't stand any more. You don't know how much you've hurt us all by what you've done. Your despair sounds dreadful, but why didn't you talk to us about it instead of—instead of trying to escape for ever. How do you think we've all been feeling? I can see why you find it easier to talk to Doctor Rogers and Charlie, but it makes us all feel so useless and guilty and jealous—' She started to cry. Alex held her; she could feel he was trembling. He said nothing. After a few moments she stood up.

'I can't bear these gnats any longer. They're eating me alive.' She began to run through the wood. When she looked around she saw Alex still sitting on the rock. His shoulders were hunched; his head was bent. She hesitated, and then went back to him and held him in her arms.

Julia arrived back home at eight-thirty, having taken a very early train. She found Rod and Lucy breakfasting, both standing up as they ate their cereal. They had not bothered to lay the table; Julia sat on the edge of it, eating an apple.

'How was Compton?'

'Good. I'm glad I stayed.'

'Dad?' Rod's question came through a mouthful.

'He's fine. I rang you last night, by the way—no reply.'

'I went to the Croxleys for supper.'

'The Croxleys?'

'Why not?'

'You wouldn't go the other night.'

'Well, I did go last night.' Rod grinned. 'It was fun. We played snooker. Then I worked all night. I haven't been to bed at all.'

'About time you started to work again. How's Charlie getting on?'

Rod spread a doorstep of bread with half an inch of butter and marmalade. 'He looked pretty miserable.'

Julia was troubled, but did not ask any more questions. She had to hurry anyway, and as soon as she reached school she sought out Carmen.

'Don't flap, Julia. Things are fine. My mother can cope with Charlie. Shouldn't think he'll stay very long with us, in fact. He seems OK to me. Hey, we had a smashing time with Rod last night. He was on fantastic form—everyone thought he was super.' Carmen chattered on, although Julia hardly listened. The last thing she needed to hear was a description of her brother's social success.

That evening, Rod was hard at work again from the moment he got home. He asked Julia to bring his supper up to his room, and disappeared. When she took the tray in, he barely looked up. She hovered, needing his company. After a while he yawned, stretched

113

and tipped his chair right back; he clasped his hands behind his head. 'What is it, Ju?'

'Nothing really.'

'Out, then. I can't stop now.'

'I just wanted to talk about Dad—'

'Well, I don't. Not one bit.' Rod sat forward and pulled his chair in, picking up his pen. Excluded, Julia left and went downstairs to eat.

She picked at her supper, and then wandered restlessly about. What she really wanted to do was go to see the Croxleys, but she had a pile of homework. She made a half-hearted attempt at it, and then decided she would definitely go to the Croxleys; after all, she might be able to help out with Charlie. Pleased she had thought of a good reason, she bicycled there immediately, only to find that Timothy, Carmen and Charlie were out.

'They've gone to the cinema,' said Amy. Julia felt pangs of angry jealousy that they hadn't thought of asking her. It was just the kind of jaunt she needed to cheer her up. Amy must have sensed her feelings because she said: 'But do come in, Julia darling. They'll be back in half an hour—they went to the five o'clock showing.' Julia followed Amy into the kitchen; she could hear Joe banging on a typewriter somewhere nearby. Amy tidied away the letter she was writing on the kitchen table. 'Actually, Julia, I'd welcome a little chat with you about Charlie. I know very little about him, and he's so reserved it's difficult to find anything out. Tell me, what's his New Zealand background?' Julia told her what she knew. 'And he's come here to finish training as a cabinet-maker.'

'How unexpected. I must talk to him about it. Perhaps I'll be able to get through to him at last. I feel at the moment he holds us all in deep suspicion.' She sighed. 'And he has such a hopeless expression in his eyes sometimes; it makes my heart bleed. I wish he would let us help him—he seems to resist all offers of help.'

'He's here, though. He didn't resist coming here.'

'Yes, he's here, thank goodness, and I will do my very best to make his stay successful. Poor Charlie, all on his own half the world away from his home.'

Julia looked surreptitiously at the kitchen clock. Ten more minutes and they would be back.

'There's another thing I'd wondered about,' said Amy, putting rice into boiling water. 'Has Charlie got a history of any mental illness? Do you happen to know?'

'Our doctor, Doctor Railton, said that as far as he and the hospital psychiatrist could see, Charlie was normal. Charlie told them this was his only suicide attempt. Doctor Railton said it was a desperate cry for help.'

'Yes, I would imagine so. Well, I'm glad they think there's no deep-seated trouble.' Amy busied herself for several minutes before going on. 'You see, I had got this strong aura of hopelessness from Charlie, as if he had no hope at all, as if he had been born without the instinct for survival, if you see what I mean.' Julia thought she did and nodded. 'But I think I must be quite wrong. Perhaps the fault lies in my approach to him, and not in his reaction.'

The phone rang; Amy picked up the kitchen extension.

'Georgina! How *nice*—how come you're in London? Oh, I see—alas, it isn't very convenient because we've got a lame duck staying—you know, one of my "lost souls" as you call them—yes, that's right, and I don't know how long for. He's an attempted suicide—I thought that would impress you. Very nice boy, and a carpenter to boot—that could be very useful.' She laughed at something her friend said. The conversation ran on, and Julia sat unhappily waiting. She was relieved when the doorbell went, and Amy said : 'Go and let them in—they never take keys.'

She flew to the front door.

'Julia! What on earth are you doing here?' Carmen bounced in.

'Nice to see you,' said Timothy, looking over her head; 'God, I need food.'

'Hullo, Julia,' said Charlie quietly. He blushed when he met her eye. 'I thought you were staying down with your grandmother.'

'I came back early this morning.'

She sat next to Charlie at the kitchen table while they all ate supper, and noticed how silent he was amidst the Croxley hubbub. If asked a direct question he would reply politely, but he never volunteered a comment of his own. At the end of the meal, when Carmen was making everyone coffee, Amy said in a pause:

'Well, Charlie, Julia tells me you're a cabinet-maker by profession.' She smiled brightly at him; Charlie looked taken aback, even aghast.

'No. Well, not yet—I'm not fully trained yet, I only did half my apprenticeship in New Zealand.'

'You've come to the right country to finish learning. There are some marvellous modern furniture makers here—Carmen, where's that craft magazine we were looking at, get it would you?—there's an article in it about John Makepeace. Perhaps you've heard of him, Charlie?'

Charlie shook his head dumbly. He was shown the article; he glanced at the photographs of cupboards, tables, chairs and chests of great beauty and design and execution. He shut the magazine, making no remark.

Amy conquered her irritation and said: 'But maybe what you're dying to do is a little carpentry work yourself? If you're interested, I've several jobs to be done—for instance, one particularly nice antique chair has come apart, and I'm sure it's worth mending. So if you feel creative, there you are. What do you think?'

Charlie nodded. 'OK. Used to do a lot of chairs.'

'I'd pay you of course—'

Charlie shook his head.

'No, no, specialist abilities are invaluable, of course I must pay you—'

'I'll do it for nothing.'

'Well, that's nice of you, Charlie.' She touched his shoulder; he stiffened.

'We're going to play poker,' declared Timothy. He fetched a pack of cards and a large box of matches which he proceeded to share out between them.

'Do you play poker, Charlie?' asked Carmen.

'Yes, I do.' He smiled suddenly. 'I used to play with my brothers.'

His unexpected participation broke the ice, and the unease he created amongst the others disappeared. Charlie was remarkably good at poker, and won continually. Amy announced at the end: 'Charlie, you're a devil. You're too good at this.'

Charlie laughed happily. He had a large pile of matches in front of him. He picked a few up and ran them through his fingers. 'I'm a millionaire.'

When Julia left, Amy followed her out of the front door conspiratorially. The others stayed inside.

'I take it back—there's hope for Charlie yet. If he's good at poker, he'll surely be able to bluff his way through life. He really blossomed this evening, didn't he?'

'Yes.'

'We must organize some more poker games.'

'Yes.'

'Now come on, Julia, you enjoyed it too. And you must make a special effort with Charlie, and try to encourage him. I could see this evening how much you in particular mean to him—much more than anyone else. He obviously likes you.'

'I'm not sure he does.' Julia finished unlocking her bicycle, and put a foot on the pedal. Amy spoke roughly. 'Oh yes, he does. And he needs you. He's someone in trouble, he needs a girl to take an interest in him, and right now you're the girl. It will make all the difference to his recovery, I'm sure of that. I was watching him watching you. You must try to be extra nice to him. It won't cost you much, but it will mean a great deal to Charlie.'

Julia flicked her bicycle lamp on and off, her fingers desperate. 'Oh God. It's not as easy as that.'

'When does your mother get back?'

'Early next week. She's going to ring again.'

'Well, you come and have all your meals here this weekend. All three of you if you like.' Amy was firm. 'Julia, you can be Charlie's lifeline, and don't you forget it.'

Julia was not convinced. 'I don't want him hanging around all the time. He might get too fond of me. We'll all be in trouble then. That would do nobody any good.'

Amy looked at her reflectively. 'It's a risk. But I would guess that he needs to give and receive simple affection—'

'You make him sound like a puppy.'

'Well, there is a simplicity about him, isn't there? He needs to be believed in by someone he likes. He likes you. All you need to do is like him, no more.'

'He doesn't turn me on at all.'

'I don't care if he doesn't turn you on, as you put it. You must just try to hide it.'

'What are you two gassing about?' Carmen came out on the doorstep.

'Off you go, Julia. It's very late.'

'You've been plotting.'

'Oh, go to bed, Carmen. We haven't been plotting—just making a few arrangements. Goodbye, Julia; see you tomorrow.'

Amy shut the heavy front door, and the glass birds rattled. 'Go on, Carmen, go to bed. Where are you, Joe? I need a whisky.'

Julia bicycled home with the sense of dreadful heaviness growing. Amy was determined and powerful; she liked to manage people like puppets, thought Julia as she pedalled furiously. How could she pretend to feel more than just liking for Charlie when the thought of him touching her in any way made her skin crawl? If she encouraged him, he would want to touch her. Damn Amy and her theories, even if she were right. Life was too full of burdens.

9

'Hey, Julia. Are you deaf? Or has Monday been too much for you?' Rod shouted at Julia on their way home from school.

'Sorry, Rod. I was thinking.'

'Don't strain yourself. You're not used to it. What's the problem, anyway?'

'Charlie.'

'Not again.'

'Amy Croxley is convinced that his only route back to ordinary life and sanity is me.' She expected derision from Rod but he was silent. 'She says I mean something special to him.'

'Do you?'

'I don't know. Maybe. Amy says I must make an effort to be nice to him, and see as much as I can of him while he's staying with them.'

'Dangerous,' said Rod at last.

'My reaction too.'

'But one shouldn't stop doing things for people just because it's dangerous. Should one?'

'Exactly, Rod. It sounds so mean to say : I won't be friendly with you in case you get too dependent on me.'

'On the other hand—'

'On the other hand.' They rode their bicycles on in silence for a while, before Julia went on : 'Amy Croxley has asked us all to supper again tonight.'

'You go. I really have to get on with my revision.'

'I wish you'd come. She'll begin to think you hate them.' Rod had not gone to the Croxleys at all over the weekend.

'I mustn't – don't try to persuade me. Take old Lucy with you for moral support.'

'You must be joking.'

When they got home, they saw that the front door was slightly open.

'Lucy must be home already.' Julia looked at Rod.

'Or Josie left it open by mistake.' Rod pushed the front door fully open, and they both saw the suitcase. 'Mum's back.'

On the kitchen table was a carrier bag containing flotsam—driftwood pieces of smooth shapes, dried seaweed purses, pebbles. Julia sniffed the bag. 'Sea smell.' Somehow the contents of the carrier bag gave her confidence that her mother's trip had been a success. Relief filled her even before Nell came quickly into the house down the garden, full of pleasure at seeing them. She hugged them both.

Rod was holding up a piece of driftwood.

'Isn't that beautiful? I spent hours just walking along the beach.' Nell picked out a piece of hardened seaweed; Julia took it and licked its saltiness.

'Well, come on, Mum, tell us—did you have a good time?' said Rod.

'Yes, yes, I did. Do you know that this was the first time I'd been on my own anywhere since Alex and I got married. Twenty years of doing things in company. It felt strange to have no one else to think about.'

'Is that why you came home early?'

After a silence, Nell answered : 'No, I came home early because I began to feel very guilty about you three.'

'You shouldn't have. We've managed fine.'

'I know, but once I started feeling guilty that was it. I made myself stay on, but the fun went.'

'Silly Mum.'

'I sat on a rock yesterday and watched the water lapping, and thought : those poor children, they've been knocked sideways by events just as much as I have. How could I have deserted them? And yet when I left to go away it seemed the right and proper thing to do.'

'It was,' said Rod firmly. 'You got better, didn't you? If you'd stayed here, you'd still be near the end of your tether.'

The telephone rang, and Nell promptly went back into the garden, saying as she went: 'Unless it's Alex, I'm not back yet.' But it was Amy, asking Julia how many were coming to supper.

'Well, actually Amy, I don't think any of us are because my mother has just this minute got back unexpectedly. So many thanks, but we'll stay here with her.'

'Of course you will. How nice to have her back.'

'Thank you for being so kind to us.'

'It was a pleasure.'

There was a short pause. 'I was going to tell you when you came round, but I'll tell you now instead. I have got some tickets for Saturday for you and Carmen and Charlie and perhaps Rod if he'd like to—Tim will have gone by then—to go to the new rock musical which I'm told the young are all mad about. I hope you can both manage it.'

'Oh. Yes, thank you very much. I'll ask Rod if he can. Is it for *Sun-Strike*?'

'That's right. Carmen seemed to think it was the show to see.'

Julia took down the details; she very much wanted to see *Sun-Strike* but not with Charlie. She had seen Charlie all weekend, and become increasingly aware of his dog-like devotion to her. She did not really know how to cope with it. However, there was no gainsaying Amy, and after persuasion Rod agreed to go as well. At least Saturday was five days off, and she would have a rest from Charlie in between.

But she reckoned without Charlie. He came to see her, that very evening.

Charlie in their house: Julia felt invaded; she had never expected him there. Charlie came in smiling awkwardly.

'Hope I'm not disturbing you.'

'Oh, not a bit,' said Nell warmly. 'Let's all have a drink—cider or beer?' Glasses and bottles were fetched.

'I like your bird and cage.' Charlie was gazing at it, fascinated.

'It's beautiful, isn't it? Lucy was given it by her grandmother. Wind it up, Lucy, and let Charlie hear the bird sing.'

Charlie sat wordless and entranced as the bird sang and sang, moving its head jerkily from side to side at intervals. Lucy, pleased with its success, wound it up again.

'I've never seen anything like it, ever.' Charlie put his large hands out towards the cage as if to pick it up, then stopped.

'It's Victorian,' said Lucy.

Charlie knelt by the cage, examining it carefully. 'Don't you like it, Julia?'

'Yes. Yes, I do. The song gets a bit repetitive though.'

'It's great.' He watched the bird reach its final trill. 'Better than real birds. It's lovely.' The word lovely sounded strange from Charlie, and his enthusiasm was unexpected too. Julia's irritation with him faded.

'How's Alex, Mrs Parrish?'

'Coming back tomorrow. Everything is getting back to normal. The nightmare is over.' She smiled warmly at him, including him in her remark.

Charlie looked straight at Nell. 'I don't think the nightmare will ever be over for me.'

'Oh, Charlie. Don't say that. And I'm sure it's not true.'

'I make such a mess of living, Mrs Parrish. I'm so bad at being with people. I never know what to say. Or do.' Charlie looked at Julia, and then back at Nell. The bird sang busily; even its pauses were busy. Charlie turned his gaze at the cage, and as he watched the bird stopped. 'I feel like a block of wood when I'm with the Croxleys. They're nice folk, but I bore them, I know I do; I can't help it.'

Nell took his hand and held it. 'Charlie, Charlie.' Her eyes were full of sympathy; her warmth and interest had sparked off his outburst. 'You mustn't think that. You don't give yourself a chance.'

'I do bore them. Don't I, Julia? They try to hide it.' Julia was tongue-tied. Charlie went on, 'I don't know why I'm telling you this, Mrs Parrish. The other Mrs Parrish scared me, but you don't. I could tell you anything.'

'Call me Nell, for goodness sake. Charlie, you must stop *thinking* you are boring. When anyone does that—and we all do it at times —we become boring. Do you sit and think about yourself a lot?'

'All the time. I'm such a mess.'

'Stop saying that, Charlie. And you must stop brooding about yourself too. It never helps.'

Julia interrupted. 'It's easy enough to say that, Mum, but we all think about ourselves—I do it all the time too. I don't see how one can help it.'

'Your mind's got to be somewhere when you're awake,' said Charlie. There was a silence. Lucy wound the bird up again but Nell stopped her playing it.

'You don't have to stay on at the Croxleys if you're unhappy there, Charlie,' said Nell at last. 'I'm sure Mrs Croxley would understand if you said you were ready to stand on your own two feet now.' Nell topped up his beer mug.

'It doesn't matter where I am, Mrs Parrish—Nell. I'm not any more unhappy or useless at the Croxleys than I would be anywhere else. As for standing on my own two feet—' he looked down at his enormous canvas boots and pulled a face. 'They're big enough.'

'Don't say you're useless,' said Julia. 'My father told me how much you helped him in hospital.'

Nell was about to ask what she meant, when they heard Rod running down the stairs. He came in stretching. 'I hear voices; who's here? Oh, hullo, Charlie.' He poured himself some beer.

Charlie froze; all his trusting openness became a confused mumble. He knocked an ashtray off the table as he moved his glass to make space for Rod's. His ears went red as he picked up the mess.

They all talked stiffly, the confiding ease quite gone. Rod reached for a newspaper to check the time of a television programme, saying as he did so : 'Do you mind, but I particularly wanted to see the film about splitting the atom.'

Charlie stayed on, watching the film with shifting attention. Julia noticed he spent several minutes with his eyes shut, his mouth taut. He left as soon as the film was finished. When he was gone, Rod said : 'What a wet blanket Charlie is.'

'You're so wrong.' Nell was angry. 'He was being absolutely sweet until you came in, wasn't he, girls; relaxed and easy-going and interesting. Then you arrived and for some reason he turned into a clumsy awkward bore.'

'I wasn't rude or unpleasant to him. What's biting him? Why should I have such a catastrophic effect on him?'

'To be fair, I don't think Charlie was reacting to you personally, but to what he thinks you stand for.'

'What do you mean—what do I stand for?'

'As far as he's concerned, you're like the Croxleys—successful, clever, fun, etcetera, etcetera.' Rod snorted. 'No, seriously, Rod. Charlie is beyond coping with success at the moment. You must deal gently with him.' Nell spoke with affection.

'Listen, Mum, if I suddenly become too understanding and friendly he'll get suspicious, and clam up even more. There's little I can do about it.' Rod looked annoyed. 'I'm becoming fed up with Charlie anyway, he's getting under everyone's skin.'

'Well, he senses that, and it only makes everything worse. His life is a vicious circle.' Nell began to collect glasses together on to the tray. 'I think it's a significant move that he came to see us tonight in the way he did.'

'So do I.' Julia spoke flatly, lying back in her chair with her eyes shut and a frown on her forehead.

'I'm sorry my arrival put such a damper on him.'

Julia hurried home after school the next day; she saw Connie's car parked outside the gate, and doors open everywhere; she felt a surge of joy and ran. She found Alex standing gloomily in the hall surveying the damaged ceiling.

'I must say, that rather spoils my homecoming,' he was saying. 'How maddening of you, Lucy. You must have had the bath on at full tilt to cause so much damage.' Lucy looked miserable. Connie broke in briskly. 'Now come on, Alex dear, don't spoil your arrival by worrying about a mere collapse of fabric.'

They all laughed, partly at her choice of phrase and partly at her tone of voice. Alex shook a mock fist at Lucy, then kissed her and Julia. 'No Rod yet? Our family routine has become so unfamiliar I will have to re-learn the pattern of the week.'

Alex picked up a suitcase, and smiled round at them. 'I rather like this unfamiliar feeling.' He started up the stairs.

'Tea,' said Nell.

'Soon.' They heard him humming as he moved about between study and bedroom. The tea was cold by the time he appeared, but he liked cold tea. Julia noticed that for once it did not annoy Nell that he drank his tea cold. It was too much to expect this mellowness to last, but it was pleasant just the same. They saw Connie off home again, and then Alex insisted that they all went and sat down in the evening sunlight in the garden; as they did so Rod arrived home and joined them.

'You look exhausted, Rod.'

'Take it as a good sign. I've been up half the night recently, working.' Rod was cheerful, and Alex looked relieved.

'It's pointless saying don't overdo it, I suppose.'

'That's right.' Rod grinned.

'Tell me, how is my friend Charlie getting on at the Croxleys?' Alex turned to Julia. 'Is he happy there?'

'Sort of.'

'Sort of?'

'He's a little out of his depth, I think,' said Nell.

'Then he shouldn't stay on there.'

'I don't think he's quite ready to live on his own yet. He's still a bit nervous of taking the plunge.' Nell spoke gently.

'I don't blame him. But he could come here for a while, couldn't he? I don't see why the Croxleys should put him up.'

Panic overcame Julia. It would be disastrous for Charlie to live with them; all the ground gained would be lost. She looked pleadingly at her mother. No one spoke; obviously Rod's thoughts were explosive from his expression. Then Nell said, still speaking in gentle tones : 'I have thought of it. But to be honest, Alex, I think we'll be more support to him at one remove, so to speak. As long as he feels he can come and see us whenever he likes, this would be more valuable than actually living with us. In the long run, he'll get more strength from that.'

'Perhaps you're right.'

'I'm sure she's right.' Rod's vehement comment showed more of his feelings than he realized.

'Don't you like Charlie, Rod? I've got a lot of time for him, but I can see he isn't everyone's cup of tea. For some reason Connie couldn't get on with him either. And as soon as I'm back in harness, I'll do my best to fix him up with an apprenticeship. Obviously his relative in Lowestoft is absolutely useless. In fact, I wrote to her about Charlie only yesterday, hoping to prick her conscience into helping him out financially if in no other way. I also wanted to write to Charlie's parents, but he didn't want me to.'

'They might not like us interfering,' said Nell.

'Precisely what Charlie himself said. He didn't mind me writing to his aunt. She visited him once in hospital, and suggested then that he went back to Lowestoft to stay with her when he came out.' Alex smiled wryly. 'I think it was the awful thought of going to Lowestoft as much as anything that made him accept our help. As you've probably noticed, he doesn't much like being helped. He doesn't refuse it, he just ignores the offer.' He stretched in his deckchair, and sighed. The evening sun had dropped behind the house and the patio was in shadow now. Petals from the climbing rose against the house lay in drifts at their feet. 'I must say, it is good to be here.'

There was silence, and then Nell went in to start preparing food. Julia sat, half day-dreaming, half thinking. She became aware that the chair Alex sat in was the one in which they had found him unconscious. Rod caught her eye; he had obviously seen the same thing, and they smiled faintly at each other.

10

'What's the matter, Charlie?' Julia was sitting beside Charlie in the bus on the way to the theatre. Carmen and Rod were several seats away. 'You look low.'

'Aw, nothing.'

'It can't be nothing. What's upset you?'

After a long pause he said : 'That bloody Amy.'

'What's she done?'

'She's not straight. She leads you on but it's all talk.' Charlie swallowed. 'I found this box of tools, see, and I was sorting them out so I could do her chair for her. She comes along and yells at me—what am I doing, what's all this mess, and when I tell her she says, oh that old chair, it's not worth mending. Chuck it out. And off she goes. Bloody woman.'

'Had you started work on the chair?'

'Took it to pieces. It could make a decent chair again.'

'Never mind, Charlie. It's her loss. Had you made a lot of mess in fact?'

'Well, I had everything laid on the kitchen floor. She never gave me a chance.'

Julia sighed. 'She's like a steamroller.'

'You're right there.'

When they reached the theatre, Carmen discovered that despite being constantly reminded, she had left the tickets behind. Rod groaned in despair and nearly went home; but because the theatre had a record of postal bookings, all was well. By this time the show had started, and they had to wait at the back for the first number to end. All four were tense; Carmen because Rod was taking no notice whatever of her, Julia because Rod was bad-tempered and Carmen was irritating; and Charlie was just tense. In the first interval they stayed in their seats, hardly talking to each other. They decided to go out for the second interval, and as they pushed their way through the foyer Rod saw a friend and disappeared to talk to him. Carmen stood beside Julia biting the corner of her programme, obviously upset.

'Who's Rod with?'

'No idea.'

'He's not in the best of moods.'

'Take no notice of him, Carmen.'

'Don't worry, I won't. It's a fantastic show, isn't it?'

'Marvellous.' Julia turned to ask Charlie what he thought of it, but at the moment he was jostled by a party of people, and in avoiding them he stepped heavily on Carmen's foot. She gave a screech of pain.

'For heaven's sake, Charlie—'

'Sorry, those people—'

'Damnation, my tights are ripped to pieces. You might be more careful. Ouch,' she rubbed her foot angrily, 'I bet I have an enormous bruise.'

Though it was obvious that her rage was increased by her frustrated feelings over Rod, Charlie looked utterly crushed.

'Oh, shut up, Carmen. It's not the end of the world. Don't exaggerate. I can't think why you wear tights in this heat anyway,' said Julia.

Carmen stormed off to the ladies' cloakroom to remove the offending tights. Julia turned to Charlie.

'I wish Carmen would stop over-reacting. It's so boring.'

Charlie was staring desperately into space. 'I think I'll go now,' he said. 'I can't stand any more.'

'Don't be ridiculous, Charlie. Take no notice of Carmen—she's not really mad at you; it's Rod she's angry with—'

'It's been a bad day.' He refused to meet her eyes. 'I feel a bit battered.'

'You can't go home in the middle like this. You'll miss the rest of the show—'

'I don't mind. I'm not enjoying it much, to tell you the truth.'

'I thought you were. It's super.' Julia wanted to shake him, as well as Rod and Carmen. 'Come on, Charlie. Cheer up. You shouldn't let Carmen upset you like this.'

'It isn't just Carmen.'

'Please don't go now. I'd be sad if you went, Charlie.'

He was silent for half a minute and then, his eyes still turned fixedly away, blurted out: 'It's no good trying to help me. I can't seem to join in your fun. I'm not the same sort of human being as you all.'

'Charlie, you've got yourself in a state again. You're talking nonsense.' Julia put her hand on his arm. In the distance she saw Carmen's cross face approaching. 'Please don't go home now. Please. For my sake.'

At last he met her eyes. His were full of pain, but his whole expression was resolved. 'It's for your sake I'm going.' He too saw Carmen. 'Goodbye. Thanks for caring.' He hurried off through the thickest part of the crowd.

'Where's Charlie off to?'

'Home. He's—he's not feeling well.'

Carmen exploded. 'Well if that isn't the limit. Honestly, I could scream. What a party.'

Julia was watching the back of Charlie's head as it disappeared. She felt his pain, and she knew she should not have let him go off on his own. But what could she have done? Should she follow him now? She took a step after him.

'Sorry about deserting you, girls.' Rod came up beside them. When he saw his sister's face he asked: 'What's the matter?'

'Charlie's just gone off. He was upset about something. I feel dreadful about letting him leave like that.'

'Which way did he go?'

She pointed, and Rod hurried off to try and catch him. Julia and Carmen followed as far as the stairs.

'Did he go off because I shouted at him?' Carmen looked uneasy.

'Not entirely. It helped.' Julia was cool.

Rod returned panting, without Charlie. 'I couldn't see him

anywhere; I had a good look up and down the street, but he had gone.'

'There goes the bell. Surely he'll be all right. I think you're fussing unnecessarily, Julia. As far as I'm concerned, it's rude of him to buzz off like that.' Carmen was defensive. They followed her to their seats, and enjoyed the last part of the show rather less than the rest.

When they reached the Croxleys' house, Charlie was not there, nor had there been any sign of him. Amy had hot dogs ready for them all. She was distressed when they told her of Charlie's departure.

'For goodness sake, didn't one of you try to stop him going off on his own like that?'

'He was with Julia when he left,' began Carmen.

'I begged him not to go,' said Julia miserably.

'But I don't understand why he wanted to leave in the first place,' said Amy angrily. 'What a waste of a ticket. Didn't he like the show?'

'It wasn't that.' Julia said no more.

'Where did he say he was going, Julia?'

'He didn't say anything. I took it for granted he would be coming back here.'

Amy went to the phone and in silence dialled a number. 'Mrs Parrish? So sorry to bother you, but I just wondered whether Charlie was with you by any chance? He apparently left the theatre early for reasons best known to himself; the other three have arrived back, but there's no sign of Charlie. No, I don't think there's anything to worry about—I'm sure he'll turn up soon. I just wanted to check whether he was with you.' After she rang off, Carmen said:

'Now you've put the wind up her as well. Everyone will be in a great Charlie-flap.'

'Look, my girl, stop criticizing everything I do and say. OK?' Amy's face was tense and flushed. 'I've had just about as much as I can take in the last few days.' She picked up her glass of wine and spilt some as she drank. Rod and Julia stood in the kitchen doorway; she motioned them impatiently to the table. 'Do sit down, you two. Have a hot dog.' She took a piled dish out of the oven, and they helped themselves in silence. Carmen said in an undertone to her mother :

'Isn't Dad back yet?'

'No, he damned well isn't. No one seems to know where he is.'

'Are you sure the paper hasn't sent him off on some story?'

'Of course I'm sure.' Amy ignored Rod's and Julia's presence. She had obviously drunk a fair amount of wine, because her actions and speech were clumsy. 'It's the usual old story. He's gone off for a fling with his dear Veronica. He'll be back tomorrow as if nothing's happened.'

Rod and Julia sat still, distressed at hearing about such painful family problems. Carmen chewed her hot dog calmly before saying : 'Don't get so steamed up about it, Mum. Joe always says we must learn not to be possessive about the people we love.'

Amy leant against the dresser, her eyes shut. 'I don't want to talk about it any more.'

The phone rang. Amy did not move, so Carmen answered it. Julia prayed it would be Charlie.

'Dad!' Carmen screeched. 'Quick, it's a long distance call from Paris.'

Amy grabbed the receiver. 'What the hell are you doing in Paris? Oh. Yes, I see. Well of course I was worried. Anyway—yes. Fine. Except Charlie has disappeared. One problem after another.' They talked on until they were cut off in mid-sentence. Amy refilled her glass, and said to Rod : 'No doubt Charlie will now ring and say he's in Timbuktu.'

'I think we ought to telephone the police,' said Rod, his face expressionless.

'I think that's a bad idea. He may turn up at any moment and it would sap his morale if he knew that the police were out looking for him.' Amy ate two hot dogs in quick succession. 'Have another, Julia.'

'I'm not very hungry, thanks.'

Amy flopped down into a chair. 'Well, at least I've heard from my errant husband.' She smiled hazily at them, flicking her fingers against her glass. Ping, ping, ping. Julia was reminded of her mother clicking the catch of her bag. She could not wait to leave the Croxleys' house.

Next day Charlie did not reappear, nor did he get in touch. In the evening Amy went round to the Parrishes to ask their advice. 'I don't want to fuss him and chase after him if he really needs to be by himself now. On the other hand, I couldn't bear him to think that we didn't care enough about him to find out how he was.' She looked pale and tired. 'I'm very surprised he hasn't got in touch with you at all. He's so attached to Julia.'

'Part of me feels we ought not to worry too much,' said Nell slowly. 'I can understand that he needs a period by himself—'

'Oh, of course, absolutely—'

'—but it's funny he hasn't been in touch. After all, he must realize what we are frightened of.'

There was silence. Alex eventually broke it. 'If he's decided he can cope with life on his own, it may not have occurred to him that we might fear otherwise; if he's decided he can't cope after all, he wouldn't want anyone to know, this time, until it was too late.'

'I think we ought to go straight to his room and see if we can find him,' burst out Julia. 'I've wanted to do that all day.'

'You may be right,' said Amy.

'Alex darling, what do you think?'

'I think we ought to do nothing.' Everyone in the room stared at him. 'I think Charlie needs our respect. He has had the strength to detach himself and go away; he has not got in touch, so he clearly doesn't want us around. Let's respect that.'

'If only we could be sure,' said Nell.

Alex looked at her worried face, and shrugged. 'We can't be sure. But my gut reaction is : leave him alone.'

'Out of all of us, you ought to know.' Rod spoke in an odd voice, but no one appeared to notice.

'I still think we ought to try and contact him. Even just a friendly note.'

'I rather agree with Julia. If you want me to do anything, I'll willingly do it.' Amy stood straightening her long cotton skirt which had splodges of paint and varnish on it. 'But I do get the feeling he doesn't like me much, so I'm probably not the right person actually to see Charlie.'

When she had gone, Nell said : 'I'm cross with Charlie. We've all been good to him, and it's very rude of him to go off like this. I shall tell him so.'

'If you get a chance.' As Rod spoke, the telephone rang, and they all gazed at it. But it was a business colleague of Alex's, ringing up to find out how he was.

'I'm fine. I'm coming in tomorrow. No, no, it's time I got back to work. Yes, indeed, see you then. Goodbye.' He rubbed his hands together.

'I thought you were going to give yourself a few more days at home,' said Nell as lightly as she could.

'No point. I don't need them. What I do need is to start work. Come on everyone, no more glooms. I suggest a game of mah-jong.' He made Nell, Julia and Rod play, though he in fact was the only one who enjoyed the game.

Julia agonized inwardly over Charlie. When she went up to bed, she sat trying to remember exactly what he had said at the theatre, and how he had looked. But this made her no wiser about his whereabouts or state of mind; he had left no clues. She got up out of bed, half wanting to talk to Rod; but she changed her mind, aware that his lack of rapport with Charlie would colour his opinions.

'Dear God, don't let him kill himself. Please keep him safe.' She found herself praying for Charlie as she had never prayed for anyone before.

Alex was in splendid form next morning; the prospect of returning to work clearly cheered him. Conversation at breakfast was animated; only as he was leaving the kitchen did Alex say to Julia : 'I can see by the look in your eye you're plotting something. If it's a visit to Charlie, then don't. The more I think about it the surer I am we ought to leave him in peace.'

'I'm not planning to see him.'

'Good. You were brooding and I wondered.'

'Don't worry.' In fact, Julia had decided that the best thing to do was to go and see Charlie's landlady. She would surely know if Charlie had been back. Julia's only problem was how and when to go.

She sat slumped at the kitchen table, wondering if she would really have the courage to go to Charlie's address on her own, when it came to the point.

'Julia—you're really worried about Charlie, aren't you?' said Nell.

'I feel we're taking the easy way out by leaving him alone.'

'Alex is so insistent. He always says women are too much in a hurry to interfere. Perhaps I'll ring up Doctor Railton and ask his advice.'

'Please don't, Mum. I'm sure it wouldn't help. He's a busy doctor—what does he care about Charlie who isn't even his patient?'

'Maybe you're right. Let's hope by the time you get home we'll have good news of Charlie.'

But there was no news at all. Julia gazed at her parents (Alex had come home early) and exploded: 'We *must* go and see him, just to show we care. If no one else is going to go, then I'll go on my own now. I remember the address perfectly.' Julia made for the door.

'I'll take you.'

She turned and looked at Alex in surprise. 'You were against it—'

'I've changed my mind. It can't do much harm, and it may do a lot of good.'

Rod put his mug down. 'I hope you manage to sort out this time-consuming business once and for all. Now I must go and work.'

As he passed the phone it rang; he lifted the receiver and found it was Amy.

'No, no news. The plan now seems to be to pay a visit to Charlie. My father has changed his mind. Yes, fine, I'll ask them.' Rod rang off, and shouted: 'Amy says would you ask Charlie what he wants done with his things.' He thundered up the stairs, muttering about the impossibility of working with all this flap going on.

'How far are Charlie's digs?' asked Alex.

'It took Granny and me about half an hour to get there, perhaps more, but you know how slowly she drives.'

'Let's go now then.'

'Do you mind if I change out of my uniform first? I feel such a twit in these clothes.'

'Whatever you like.' Alex sat down again. He looked tired and low-spirited.

Upstairs, Julia realized that with the sudden removal of opposition to her desire to contact Charlie, she now felt worried and unsure about it. Her doubts grew as she put on the first clothes that came to hand. She went into Rod's room.

'Rod, do you think it's mad to go after Charlie—'

Rod pushed his chair back. 'Look, I have no interest in Charlie whatever. None. I couldn't care less if he's jumped in the lake. Wish he would. I am *fed up* with all this tension and emotion. I've got work to do which my future depends on.'

Julia left the room in a hurry. Near to tears, she went back to her own room, and gazed at herself in the mirror. Her shirt was awful, it made her look like a pudding. She took it off and put another one on that fitted better; but it did not match her skirt. She searched for her old denim skirt, but it was in the wash.

'Julia! What on earth are you up to? Come on!'

So she wore the skirt that did not go with her shirt and hurried downstairs. Nell looked sideways at her odd combination of clothes but said nothing. They set off, and Alex asked Julia about the house where Charlie lived.

'With the landlady in the basement, we might not need to see Charlie at all.' Something in her father's tone told Julia that he was nervous of talking to Charlie. She herself did not particularly want to see Charlie, but instinct told her that she must. After a pause, she said : 'How did it go today at work, Dad?'

'Not too badly. I've got out of the habit of being near lots of people—I felt quite claustrophobic in the canteen. There was an enormous backlog of sheer administration, and that rather overwhelmed me too. But then I didn't expect it to be otherwise. Picking up the threads after a break is always hard going. But one good thing happened : I found a letter from a furniture firm suggesting I start a local scheme for apprentices. Could be perfect for Charlie.'

They said no more until they reached Charlie's street. Alex parked the car some way from the right house. Then they both stayed sitting until Alex said :

'We're a pair of cowards. Come on, let's go.' He got out quickly and Julia followed.

'His landlady was called Mrs Grayson, I think. The entrance to the basement is here.' They went down the steep steps into a paved area full of dustbins and rusty pipes untidily piled. A cat shot noisily across them while they waited for someone to answer the doorbell. Joan Grayson came to the door with a child in pyjamas on her hip. Sounds of other children arguing came clearly from inside the flat. Alex smiled as charmingly as he could.

'Good evening. Mrs Grayson? I'm so sorry to disturb you at what must be the children's bedtime.' Mrs Grayson was staring frostily at them both. 'I'm Alex Parrish—you've met Julia before. We've come in search of Charlie Brenan.'

'You needn't have troubled yourselves.' Mrs Grayson, though untidy and tired-looking, had beautiful dark blue eyes, and these were full of hostility. She put down the child, and said : 'Go inside, there's a good boy.' She leant against the doorjamb, and lit a half-cigarette she had in her top pocket.

'Is Charlie here?' Julia asked. 'If he's not, I don't know what we'll do. I've been counting on his being there.'

'Maybe he's here, maybe he's not. What did you want of him?'

'Just to find out if he's all right. You see, I was the last person to talk to him before he went off—'

Alex interrupted. 'All we need is reassurance about his well-being, Mrs Grayson. We aren't here to interfere.'

'He came back late Saturday night. He said he never wanted to see any of you again.'

'*Any* of us?' cried Julia.

Mrs Grayson did not reply at once; as she wrapped her arms round her skinny body, Julia noticed how yellow her index and third fingers were from nicotine. 'He says he hates the lot of you and the next minute he's saying things about you—' she jerked her head at Julia—'as if he's in love with you. Julia this and Julia that. Then he says he never wants to see any of you again. But we all say one thing and mean the opposite. Give him time. He hasn't had long to get used to the fact that he tried to kill himself and it didn't work out.'

'Yes,' said Alex. 'I realize that.'

'He was down here earlier, talking to me for hours while the kids were at school.' She paused, but did not elaborate. 'One of his problems is that he's left all his stuff with that other family, and he says he can't face going to get it. He asked me to ask my husband if he'd go. Tim's got a van, and I don't suppose he'd mind, but he's not back yet so I haven't had a chance to ask him.'

'Please don't bother your husband; we'll bring Charlie's gear over for him. That'll be easy.' Alex hesitated, and then went on : 'Mrs Grayson, do you have any idea how he is off for money? I don't mean to pry, but being penniless could add to his mental strain, and he's had enough of that recently.'

'He's always paid his rent promptly; he's good about his little debts too, milk and such. But he doesn't talk about money, so I've never asked him. He's a funny chap, very secretive in some ways.'

Julia rolled a pebble under her sandal, back and forth, in the silence that followed.

'What shall we do?' said Alex dismally.

'I think I ought to go up and see Charlie, despite what he said to Mrs Grayson.'

'Shall I come with you?'

'Let her go on her own. She's the one Charlie likes. He'll be too pleased to see her to chuck her out.'

Alex laughed ruefully. 'I expect you're right. I'll go and wait in the car, Julia.'

'Don't do that. Come inside and wait here if you like.' Mrs Grayson had obviously taken to Alex; he, too, found her edgy friendliness sympathetic.

'That's very kind.'

'Come in then, and don't mind the mess. Like a cup of coffee?'

'Very much, thank you.'

As Julia climbed the area steps the battered, almost paintless basement door shut behind her father. She felt very much on her own as she went round to the front of the house. The front door was opened by entry-phone; and just as she was wondering what to do, because she was sure Charlie would not admit her if he had time to choose, the door opened and she was able to slip in as someone came out. She climbed the stairs, only vaguely remembering on which floor Charlie's room was. She eventually found the door with the label in mirror-writing and quailed at the prospect of knocking on it. She listened outside; there was a slight sound of movement in the room, like a chair being shifted, then silence again. Julia nearly turned and went down the stairs to fetch Alex, but a burst of laughter and talk from the room behind her gave her courage. She knocked twice.

'Is that you, Joanie?' Charlie's footsteps came to the door.

'No. It's me, Julia.'

Silence.

'Charlie, it's Julia.'

'What do you want?'

'I—I just came to see how you were getting on.'

'I'm getting on fine.' There was no movement from behind the door at all.

'Charlie, please open the door and let me in. Please.'

Charlie unlocked the door and opened it slightly. When he saw Julia he smiled despite himself, and opened it wider. She smiled too, though she felt tears pricking at the back of her eyes. She swallowed, unable to speak. Charlie looked pale, and had not shaved, so his heavy dark growth of beard made him seem older, different.

'Hi. Come in. Sorry about the reception.' Julia walked past him into the room, and he closed the door after her and locked it. Then he unlocked it again, and smiled sheepishly.

Julia had remembered the room as infinitely depressing. It was changed; only by small things, but changed nonetheless. Charlie had put his few possessions out, and a side light gave a warm glow. Outside the uncurtained open window the fading sunset echoed the glow. There was a pleasant smell of bacon and eggs, and by the signs of dishes on the floor, Charlie had just eaten his supper. He offered her a cup of instant coffee; his own was steaming beside a chair.

'Thanks, Charlie. I'd love some.' She thought of her father drinking coffee two floors below, but did not mention him.

'Have a seat. The seat.'

'What about you?'

'I'll sit on the bed.' But he stayed leaning against the chest of drawers, and rubbed his bristly chin.

'Afraid I look a mess, but I left my things at the Croxleys.'

'We're going to—would you like us to bring them all over for you? We could easily.'

'No, it's fine, thanks. I've made arrangements for the stuff to be collected.'

There was a tense silence. Julia saw pitfalls all around, and wondered how on earth she would avoid them. Charlie stiffened uneasily and went to open the window. He was wearing old jeans and an equally tattered T-shirt. She looked at his broad shoulders and bent head and took a deep breath.

'You didn't miss much the other night, Charlie. The show wasn't nearly as good at the end.'

'Oh.' He moved towards the electric kettle, now boiling, and started to make her coffee. 'Strong, medium or weak?'

'Fairly strong, please.'

'Strong it is.' He put a full teaspoonful of coffee into a mug, and then peered into the jar. 'Not much left. I must remember to get some.'

Julia noticed his own coffee was weak, and felt bad about using up his supply. 'Thanks, Charlie. That looks perfect.' He now sat down on the bed, and sipped from his own mug. 'I must do a proper shop tomorrow, I'm running out of everything. Got out of the habit of catering for myself.'

Julia burned to offer him help of any kind, but his manner forbade it; however efficiently or inefficiently he was coping, he clearly did not want help.

'How's your nice mother?'

'She's fine. She's delighted to have Dad back in such good spirits.'

Charlie looked at his mug, but said nothing. Julia went straight to the point. 'And you, Charlie, how are you? We've been so worried about you.'

'Why worry about me? I'm all right.'

'Of course we were worried about you! How could we not be? You left without a word of warning, you didn't say where you were going. We didn't know what had become of you, and there was no call from you.' Her voice sounded shrill and indignant; she tried to speak more calmly. 'Anyone would have worried.'

Charlie got up and returned to the window. 'It was time I came back here.'

'I'm sorry we drove you away.'

'You didn't drive me away.'

'Well, the Croxleys did then. You were desperate about them.'

'Not desperate. They kept pushing me about, and running my life. I didn't see why they should; suddenly it seemed they didn't have the right to take kindness that far. My life may be a mess in their eyes, but it's my life.' Charlie clicked the window latch back and forth incessantly. His T-shirt showed damp sweat stains. 'And it is a rotten mess.'

'Your life isn't a mess, Charlie. Look at this room.'

'What do you mean?'

'I thought this room was dismal when I saw it empty, but now you're back in it, it's got warmth and—and meaning. Why do you have so little faith in yourself?'

'No one, except one old man, ever had faith in me; why should I have faith in myself? Anyway, I don't care, I've got used to it.'

'I've got faith in you. My parents have too.'

'Not your father.'

'You're so wrong there. He has a lot of time for you. He's already found a possible job for you, he told me so today. And my mother certainly has faith in you—if you haven't seen that you must be blind.'

Charlie gazed at Julia. 'I sort of had seen it.'

'Then why do you get all worked up about nobody ever having faith in you? I'm sure there are lots of people besides us who have. What about your parents?'

Charlie snorted. 'They find it difficult to believe I'm even successful at breathing, I'm such a washout in their eyes.' Then he started to laugh, his high-pitched chuckle infectious this time. Julia smiled.

'Come on, what's the joke?'

'I nearly gave them the pleasure of being right.' His chuckles subsided slowly.

'Well, isn't it satisfactory to have given them one in the eye?'

'Yes.' He came across the room and put a finger on top of her head. 'Yes, it is indeed.'

There was a knock on the door. Julia prayed it was not her father. Relief flooded through her when she heard Joan Grayson's voice.

'It's only me, Charlie. Open up.'

He opened the door a mere crack. 'I've got a friend here.'

'I'm not stopping. Just came to say Tim's back and he says he can't help you with your stuff till the end of the week. He's sorry and all that, but the van's in dock.'

'Never mind. Tell him not to bother. See you, Joan, and thanks.' He shut the door firmly.

'Please let us bring your stuff over for you, Charlie. We can drive it over from the Croxleys tomorrow evening. Dad told me to suggest it.'

Charlie thought about it before answering. 'Thanks. It would help a lot. I don't think I could bear to face a Croxley at the moment.'

'Don't worry, they don't come with the luggage.'

'Don't tell them I feel so paranoid about them.'

'Of course we won't.' Julia was beginning to feel very tired; she had drawn deeply on her mind and her heart in this conversation with Charlie, and she knew she had reached her limit.

Charlie smiled at her, and picked up something from the top of his chest of drawers. 'A present for you, Julia.' He held it out.

She stood up to see what he had in his palm; it was his jade Maori figure with its round eyes. 'Oh no, Charlie, you can't give that to me. It's precious to you.'

'Why can't I give it to you if I want to? It will bring me more luck in your possession than it ever has in mine.' He handed it to her, and she took it reluctantly.

'Let's make it a loan, Charlie. You can ask for it back any time you want to.'

'All right, if that makes you happy.'

'It does.' The charm dangled from Julia's fingers on its silver chain. 'Charlie, I must go. It's getting late and I haven't had supper yet.'

He did not seem to hear. She moved towards the door, and put her hand on the knob. 'Dad and I will bring your things round tomorrow evening. Or if Mum does it with me, we could come much earlier, around five o'clock.'

'I'd rather see your mother than Alex at the moment.'

'Then I'll come with her.' Julia opened the door slightly. 'And thanks for the charm.'

'It's less than I owe you.'

'You don't owe me anything.'

'You'll never know how much I owe you.' He stared blankly at the window. Julia pulled the door open further, unable to answer.

'See you tomorrow.'

'Yes, Charlie, see you tomorrow.'

There were tears running gently down his cheeks. She closed the door, and went down to the basement to find her father.